THE PASSION

The Hollis Sisters
Book 3

ANNABELLE MARIN

Published by Blushing Books
An Imprint of
ABCD Graphics and Design, Inc.
A Virginia Corporation
977 Seminole Trail #233
Charlottesville, VA 22901

The Passion
Annabelle Marin

eBook ISBN: 978-1-63954-537-7
Print ISBN: 978-1-63954-538-4

Chapter 1

New York City, March 1852

Helene Hollis would always be "too much" of something. Too much of a redhead. Too clumsy. Her breasts were too big for her short body. Too plain to be compared to her beautiful older sisters, Corinne and Audrina, who had secured rich, handsome husbands.

But she had two gifts. One, she was an excellent conversationalist if one gave her a chance, and two, she was an excellent dancer, unlike her older sisters. Corinne was too aggressive and Audrina would often be too lost in her own head to be able to follow the steps properly.

Though Helene had no idea if she would even dance tonight at Mr. and Mrs. Lloyd's ball given the night was more than half over and her mother, who was acting like her chaperone tonight, would more than likely tell her it was time to go home soon.

Helene let out a frustrated stomp of her navy blue high-heeled slippers while a stupid smile remained on her face. It wouldn't do any good to throw a tantrum in the middle of a large party, especially since the eighteen-year-old had just made her own debut a few weeks ago.

This was her first ball since her own debut and Helene hated to admit it, but she was disappointed. It wasn't at all what she imagined from the girlish dreams of her youth. She didn't have even one suitor and no one had bothered to fill her dance card.

The youngest Hollis sister knew she wasn't ugly, but since the rest of New York society had met her older sisters, she had to admit she had probably been a disappointment with how different she was from them physically. Corinne and Audrina had inky black hair, porcelain skin like delicate dolls, and stunning blue eyes.

Meanwhile, while Helene also had blue eyes, hers seemed less stunning, her hair was a vibrant orange red, and her skin looked more sickly than porcelain. She pressed the glass of champagne against her lips and drank to remove the sting of rejection.

Helene suddenly wished her sisters were here even though Corinne would probably steal all of the men's affections and Audrina would get asked to dance more despite her terrible dancing skills. At least she wouldn't feel so lonely.

The truth of the matter was both of her sisters were in England. Vivacious Corinne found herself married to a no-nonsense English gentleman, and the intelligent Audrina had followed her American husband overseas because he needed to conduct business.

Helene plastered a smile on her face when she saw her mother approach. Her father rarely attended balls anymore, preferring to nap or spend time in his private library. However, Mrs. Hollis was determined to attend every ball, to make sure Helene got married as soon as possible to a respectable gentleman like her sisters' husbands. Though, she had admitted, much to Helene's dismay, that she wasn't too hopeful. Her mother made it sound like she was destined to be a spinster at only eighteen.

"We're leaving in twenty minutes. I only have to say goodbye to that dreadful Mrs. Lloyd; otherwise, I will never hear the end of it." Mrs. Hollis was wearing a gray dress with stiff, lace cuffs, looking outdated against her youngest daughter's dark blue dress with the wide skirts and the cinched waist. Her mother's eyes trailed down Helene as they often did since she came out to society. "When we get home, tell Paulette to get rid of that dress. I'm sure the church can find a poor soul for it."

Helene frowned. "Why?" The dress was new; she and her mother had picked it up from the dressmaker just last week.

Mrs. Hollis shook her head. "It's all wrong. Remind me to tell Mrs. Downey not to place you in navy blue anymore. It makes your hair look even redder and you will never get a proposal at this rate. Did you gain weight again, Helene? Your bosom is practically spilling out of your bodice. It looks like you can hardly breath."

Helene turned scarlet as she looked around, afraid someone had heard, but everyone else seemed too drunk or too engrossed in their conversation to care about a mother humiliating her young daughter.

"No," Helene whispered quietly even though she knew it was a lie. She had been eating more sweets lately on account of her mother's henpecking making her nervous. Ever since her sisters had left for Europe, her mother had become more obnoxious. It didn't help that men barely looked in her direction after they discovered she wasn't as witty as Audrina or as pretty as Corinne.

Mrs. Hollis looked like she didn't believe her. She shook

her head before heading to look for the hostess. Helene relaxed only slightly. She knew the rest of the carriage ride home would just be her mother expressing her disappointment about how she couldn't even manage to have one gentleman ask her to dance.

"Helene!"

Helene turned around and saw her best friend, Kathleen Easton, walking towards her wearing a dusty pink and blue dress, with faux blue flowers in her tight brown curls. She was holding the arm of a handsome young man with matching dark brown hair, a mischievous look in his blue eyes as if he were hiding something.

The redhead immediately recognized him as Kathleen's older brother, twenty-four-year-old Zachary Easton who had recently graduated from Harvard business school after spending two years traveling through Asia.

"I'm so happy you're still here. We thought most people had left already, but I so did want to come even if Father didn't, so Zachary, being the gentleman he is, saved me from utter boredom." Kathleen squeezed her brother's upper arm happily. She tended to ramble when she was excited and Helene knew how excited she was to have her older brother home for good after having him gone for six years. Zachary was expected to take over the family's jewelry emporium.

Kathleen's mother had died when she was seven, and the girl therefore often felt lonely in the large house, with only the servants, her father, and brother for company. The two girls had quickly formed a friendship when they shared a violin tutor when they were ten.

Zachary gently elbowed his younger sister in the ribs, causing the girl to blush. "I am so sorry. I am being terribly rude. Helene, you remember my brother Zachary Easton. Zachary, Miss Helene Hollis."

Zachary gave a small bow of his head as he kissed her gloved hand. "It's a pleasure to see you again, Miss Hollis. I heard your sisters married while I was away. Congratulations."

"Thank you." Helene sucked in her cheeks, wondering why she was suddenly so nervous. This was not the first time she had interacted with Zachary, but the last couple of times they had met, she had still been in the nursery, not allowed on any fun social outings which didn't involve dolls.

Zachary was a handsome, rich, red-blooded male. Someone she could quite possibly marry. They were both unattached, after all, and there wasn't a huge difference in age between them. The thought only caused her pasty skin to turn a horrid shade of red.

Kathleen cocked her head to the side. "Hel, are you feeling well? You're all red."

Helene swayed a little in her shoes as she tried to regain her composure. "Yes, I'm fine. I apologize; the room just started feeling hot all of sudden."

"I could come with you to the garden," Kathleen offered sweetly. "Zach can be our chaperone, won't you?"

Helene spoke before Zachary could say a word. She didn't want to be treated like an annoying little sister who was too delicate. Men never married women like that.

Instead, she turned to face him, plastering a fake smile on her face. "Congratulations on finishing your studies. Are you planning on deserting us soon to continue your adventures in Asia or Europe?" She was satisfied by what she said. It sounded charming and sultry, like something Corinne might say. Her oldest sister had had many gentlemen fawn over her before she had been forced to marry her cold English gentleman.

Zachary laughed. His laugh reminded Helene of

wedding bells. "From your lips to God's ears, Miss Hollis. I'm afraid my father wants me to settle in New York for the next year at least, so he can teach me the family business. He's worried he's getting too old though he managed to send me a letter every day during my last semester at Harvard."

Helene smiled at the prospect of seeing Zachary for the next year at least. "It will be marvelous to see you around town." She realized how outspoken she sounded when Zachary started looking at her in amusement. She sounded too eager. Helene was glad it was just Kathleen with her; otherwise, gossip would flow all through New York about how Mrs. Hollis' youngest daughter was throwing herself at the Eastons' heir like some floozy. "What I meant to say is I'm sure Kathleen is eager to show you around."

Kathleen squeezed her brother's arm. "Zach is going to be my new chaperone for all of my social outings. Father is getting too old and I want to get married soon."

Zachary shook his head in a teasing way. "What is it with you American girls and your obsession with marrying? You don't see French girls thinking they're old maids the second they turn eighteen. How about you, Miss Hollis, are you like my sister and running to the altar?"

Helene fought the urge to say that if he were her groom, she wouldn't mind getting married right this second and having his babies. "Well, there isn't much for women to do besides marriage." The statement was true, after all. Perhaps if she weren't rich and didn't come from a good New York family, she would be able to work as a seamstress or perhaps run a small business. But alas, she was destined to become a wife and mother and run her own grand home just like her sisters were doing. Helene had never thought much about the what ifs. As far as she knew, it was a complete waste of time. "But, Mr. Easton, I have only recently had my debut. I am not looking for a husband just yet."

He gave her a small wink that only she could see and not his sister. "Smart lady, though I'm sure your mother wouldn't want to hear you say that."

"No, she wouldn't." Across from the Lloyd's massive ballroom, Mrs. Hollis was motioning towards her impatiently with her fan, letting her know it was time to go. "I apologize; my mother and I have to retire for the evening. It was nice seeing both of you."

Kathleen kissed her cheek. "Let's go shopping on Thursday. I need new gloves."

Helene nodded as she gave a small curtsy to Zachary while he bowed.

"Miss Hollis, will you be going to the Shepard's ball on Friday?" She nodded and he smiled. "Excellent, will you save me a spot on your dance card?"

To say that Helene Hollis was stunned, would be to put it lightly. Men seldom asked her to dance, even during her own debutante ball where she was the guest of honor. She swallowed hard, trying hard to contain her squeals. "Of course, Mr. Easton."

Once Helene reached her mother, both women were handed their coats by one of the footmen who had been put to the task. Mrs. Hollis didn't speak to her until they were in the privacy of their carriage. Her mother was not against humiliating Helene, but she never did it in public, for fear someone else would also recognize the young woman's flaws.

"Who were you conversing with? The dark-haired young man next to Kathleen?"

"Zachary Easton, he's Kathleen's older brother. He just finished his studies at Harvard and he's back in New York."

Mrs. Hollis pursed her lips. "Ah, yes, the traveler. I

never understood young men's obsessions with traveling to more uncivilized places. What place could be better than New York?"

"Well, I've heard Spain and Greece can be quite lovely. Not to mention, your daughters moved to England."

Mrs. Hollis didn't seem amused. "No dances today, Helene?"

Helene flushed red from shame as she looked at her lap where her hands were slowly turning splotchy and red. They always did when her mother was humiliating her, making her less invisible.

"No, Mother." She perked up remembering Zachary's proposal. "But Zach… I mean Mr. Easton… made me promise him a dance at the Shephard's ball in a few days."

Mrs. Hollis sighed as she settled back in the velvet seat. "I suppose it's a start, but, Helene, you should start thinking seriously about your prospects or lack of any. The last thing you need is for the years to go by and you find yourself unmarried because you let time slip away for you. There are fresh debutantes each year, all wanting the same thing—a ring on their finger and a worthy last name. It will be good for you to remember that."

"Yes, Mother, but if you recall, my sisters married after turning twenty, so there—"

"But you're not Corinne nor Audrina," her mother interrupted coldly, shaking her head. This made Helene feel like an even bigger fool. "They had the advantage of being…" *More beautiful? More charming? Better? Just say it, Mother.* "You're different from your sisters. You need to get married this year if you want to be married at all."

Helene felt numb, and her heart felt like it was shrinking in defeat the more her mother kept talking. "Perhaps, Mr. Easton—"

Mrs. Hollis laughed. "Zachary Easton is not the man for you, Helene."

"But he comes from a good family. An old one, like ours. His great-grandfather was the younger brother of a duke."

"Even so, he is not for a girl like you. Men like him have a wandering foot, they never want to settle in one place. You will be a miserable wife, left behind while he goes galivanting to foreign countries to impregnate peasant woman while you're sitting home like an idiot," Mrs. Hollis stated coldly. "It's better if he married one of the Olsen girls; they both seem to be content lusting after the servants."

Helene choked on a gasp.

"Besides, even if Mr. Easton didn't have his flaws, it is doubtful he would set his eyes on you. Perhaps Audrina would be able to enchant him with all the reading she does, but never you, my dear."

Mrs. Hollis seemed unaware of the tears that had settled in her daughter's eyes which she was trying not to let fall. "Don't worry, Helene. If you are a spinster, you can always stay with me. Someone needs to take care of me and it's not going to be your sisters."

The idea of an eternal life with her mother seemed like a sentence worse than Hell.

On the day of the Shephard's ball, Helene dressed in a pale pink dress with a dozen tiny yellow ruffles along the wide skirt. The redhead thought she looked like a walking pastry, but her mother argued she looked just darling.

She looked around the elegant ballroom for signs of Kathleen or her brother, but she didn't find them at all. The young woman had been standing there for an hour and she didn't know how much longer she could fake a smile.

Helene had dabbled in a bit of small talk with the other debutantes, but it seemed everyone but her had a dance partner who was eager to sweep them into their arms. She frowned as she looked at her empty dance card. She had been tempted to write Zachary Easton's name in pretty penmanship, but eventually, she decided against it.

Maybe he had just been polite when he saw how pathetic Helene looked and he wanted to make his little sister's best friend happy.

I was looking forward to it, she thought silently.

Her blue eyes closed as she imagined dancing with Zachary, their bodies pressed together even though most people would have thought it was inappropriate, their lips nearly touching, her skirts swinging through the elegant ballroom as they danced beautifully.

Helene's daydreaming was interrupted when she heard a crash followed by horrid gasps. She opened her eyes and stared down in horror at the young footman she had bumped into. Broken champagne glasses were on the floor, as was the golden liquid, and on the elegant uniform.

The footman who was around her age was blushing terribly. "I apologize, Miss Hollis. I was merely trying to offer you a glass of champagne."

Helene attempted to speak, but her mouth suddenly felt dry. She was growing hotter by the second, especially as the whispering continued. The redhead swore her mother was glaring at her from where she was standing.

"Miss Hollis, there you are. I believe you owe me a dance."

Helene raised her head to look at Zachary Easton who stood before her in his evening best, his chocolate brown hair swept back to show off his lovely blue eyes. He was offering his hand to her while the rest of New York society pretended to be engulfed in something else.

The music had started again as two footmen quickly attempted to clean up the broken glass from the floor. If Helene didn't want to end up as the scandal of the evening, she must pretend this whole disaster had never happened.

She placed her pale-yellow gloved hand in Zachary's larger one, surprised at how hard and masculine it felt. Zachary was a foot taller than she, making her feel impossibly small, but also protected in a way that made her feel safe.

"Yes, I do, Mr. Easton," Helene murmured as she allowed herself to be led into the center of the ballroom.

Chapter 2

"We're dancing marvelously, don't you think?"

Zachary Easton tilted down his chin to look at the grinning face of Helene Hollis. She was so small, she barely reached his chest, which made him feel like a giant as he twirled her curvy little body around the Shephard's ballroom.

Helene was a good dancer, despite the pink and yellow monstrosity she was wearing which made her look like a dessert tart. He much preferred the stunning blue gown she'd worn when Kathleen first introduced them. The gown had been much simpler and it had matched her eyes.

"You're very light on your feet. Your dress must weigh twenty pounds." He regretted the words as soon as he said them. Women were very fussy about their clothes and seldom appreciate it when men commented on them.

Much to his surprise, Helene let out a laugh as she gave a roll of her delicate shoulders. "You can blame my mother; she chose this for me to make me stand out. I much prefer something simpler."

"Like your blue dress."

She looked up at him with wonder at the simple comment. Like he was thinking, women were odd about clothes. "Like the blue dress. Thank you for saving me from embarrassment."

"I live to serve, Miss Hollis. What were you daydreaming about that you didn't see the footman in front of you?"

Helene blushed bright pink. "Oh, nothing."

Helene had hardly changed since they had been children playing in the Eastons' private garden with their nannies trailing after them, despite their age differences. When he had been fourteen, he had been sent to boarding school in Boston while Kathleen and Helene began sharing private tutors. Their childhood had ended before they had realized it and it seemed odd that Zachary and Helene were together once again.

Helene had not changed in the years he had spent away from New York ballrooms. She still had the bright red hair which reminded Zachary of sunsets and the creamy pale skin that looked soft to the touch.

"What is it?" Helene forced herself to ask, making Zachary realize he had probably stared too long. She probably thought he was being rude.

"Nothing." He smiled. "I was just thinking about how much has changed since we were children."

"I am probably still faster than you," she blurted out with a competitive gleam in her eyes.

Zachary raised an eyebrow. "Are you willing to bet on it, Miss Hollis? I'm happy to inform you I built up my stamina while I was away on my travels."

The youngest Hollis sister nodded eagerly. He had always liked her the most, out of the three. Corinne was too snobbish, and Audrina preferred to have her nose stuck in a book rather than socialize. Helene, however, had never been afraid to voice her opinion or get dirty. It was a miracle neither of them had suffered through any broken bones by how rough they had played.

"It's a bet. Please call me Helene, like you used to. You don't have to call me Miss Hollis when it's just the two of us."

"I will if you will call me Zachary. Every time someone addresses me as Mr. Easton, I turn around, expecting to see my father."

Helene giggled.

She was rather adorable, Zachary had to point out. He hoped the man who married her appreciated her humor and didn't turn her into a dull woman like the rest of society's wives. It would be shame.

"Do you miss traveling? Kathleen told me you traveled to Asia before you attended university."

"I spent some time in China and Japan. Mostly Japan."

Helene's eyes twinkled with excitement as one of his hands pressed against her lower back while the other squeezed her yellow gloved hand gently. It had been too long since he had been close to any woman besides his sister and even longer since he'd fucked someone properly. Zachary didn't like using whores unless absolutely necessary, but as he got closer to Helene and smelled the rose water which lingered on her skin and hair, he started to long for a woman.

Not Helene Hollis, of course, she was too young for him and his little sister's best friend, but he started to realized that his father was right and perhaps it was time to settle down. Zachary hoped to find himself someone like Helene, sweet and funny. Many of his friends were trapped in miserable, loveless marriages, and he hoped it was not his fate as well.

"Tell me about it, Zachary."

The only other woman who called him Zachary was Kathleen, and he had to admit it was nice to hear it from Helene's lips as well. Less formal. Less judgmental, which was a rare occurrence when one was part of one of the wealthiest families in New York. Manners and reputation always came first.

Zachary told Helene elaborate stories about his time in China and Japan. The food he ate, especially the sweets—they seemed to get Helene's attention the most because she would often ask him to describe the taste and looks of them.

Finally, the music ended, indicating the end of their dance. Helene curtsied at him while Zachary bowed, then pressed his lips to the back of her hand. "Thank you for being such a lovely dancer, Helene. I must admit it's nice to talk to a woman with sense." He led her away from the dance floor towards a loveseat where Kathleen, along with other unmarried girls, waited for offers to dance while they giggled and gossiped. "Now, I won't waste any more of your time. I'm sure you have dozen of admirers waiting to take my place."

For some reason, Helene's face fell as if he had said something insulting though Zachary was not sure what. He had thought he had complimented her. Before he could ask her what was wrong, she curtsied again before joining Kathleen on the loveseat without looking back at him.

"Your sister is pregnant."

Helene looked up from the embroidery she had been pretending to do for the past hour. Afternoons with Mother had become less enjoyable ever since Corinne and Audrina married and left her to fend for herself.

It was two weeks after the Shephard's ball and it was an unusually slow spring week which resulted in Helene being bored more often than not. Even Kathleen had given her flute lessons more priority than spending time with her friend.

"Which sister?"

Corinne and her husband, Nicholas, had a little girl named Clarissa who'd been born last year. Corinne was so vain about her figure, she doubted she would have gotten pregnant so soon even if her husband wanted another girl.

Her mother looked unusually happy, which was a rare occurrence, Mrs. Hollis had started to become vividly aware of her youngest daughter's unpopularity. After having two popular daughters, even if both of them had caused scandals, she wasn't used to dealing with a wallflower daughter.

"Both." Mrs. Hollis beamed as she handed her the letter Audrina had written. "Audrina found out shortly after they got on the ship to London. When they got there, they received the happy news that Corinne was also expecting again. I hope they both have boys. Clarissa is darling, but she can't inherit her father's estate."

"Girls are nice too, even if they can't inherit."

Mrs. Hollis ignored her as she stood up, a determined look on her face. "Well, this news just seals it. Helene, we need to get you married this year. You cannot be the only one without a baby. Why, you will be miserable."

"I'm sure I will find something to keep me entertained, Mother."

"Something sinful, no doubt," Mother murmured, her shoulders slumping. She then perked up, which Helene always took as a bad sign when it came to her mother. "An arranged marriage."

"What?"

"An arranged marriage." Mrs. Hollis' lips twitched. "They are still quite popular, especially for younger sons and daughters who do not have as many options as their older siblings. Your father and I were an arranged marriage as well as your grandparents. Why didn't I think of it before?"

"I don't want an arranged marriage," she protested, struggling to hide her fury. "I want to marry for love."

"A love match, how positively ridiculous." Mrs. Hollis scowled. "Both your sisters had arranged matches and now they have adoring husbands and babies. Are you telling me that is not what you wish? I know young, modern girls like yourself think arranged marriages are old-fashioned, but they're quite tidy. Why, European royals have them all the time."

"We are not European royals!" she snapped.

Mrs. Hollis' thin lips pinched into a grimace as she glared at her younger daughter. "One year."

"Pardon me?"

"You have one year to find a love match. If, by your nineteenth birthday, you have not acquired this perfect man you have in mind, then your father and I will choose for you."

Helene relaxed a bit. It seemed fair enough. Certainly, more than Corinne and Audrina had gotten as far as options went. "A year is a perfectly acceptable date, Mother."

Now, she only needed a gentleman to marry.

"Are gentlemen interested in me?"

The way Kathleen stopped biting her cookie was

almost comical. The girl had to take a sip of her tea to make sure she could swallow properly.

Helene tried her best not to make her face fall in disappointment. Was it really a horrible thing to ask?

"Of course, they are! You are a Hollis girl. Any gentleman would be lucky to call you his."

Despite her kind words, Helene wasn't fully satisfied. It almost felt like her friend was lying to her to protect her feelings. She knew she wasn't odious looking, but she also knew she wasn't the prettiest debutante.

"Do you know any men who would be interested in marrying me?" Helene continued trying to appear nonchalant but failed.

Kathleen bit her lower lip, avoiding her desperate eyes. She was trying to avoid telling Helene what the girl already knew. There was a reason why her dance card had been empty these past few weeks, with the exception of men her mother guilted into dancing with her.

Kathleen continued looking at her lap, fidgeting while mussing her dress. "You just debuted, Hel. There is still plenty of time for you to be successful on the marriage mart."

Helene slumped in her seat, unmoved by the way her friend was trying to comfort her. "Why don't they want to court me?"

"You hair is too red."

"What?"

"It's just what I've heard. They think your hair is too red. They're afraid their babies will come with red hair. Don't listen to them. I think red hair is beautiful; you look like a fairy."

"Anything else?"

"They think you're too outspoken. You say what's on your mind, blurt it almost. It doesn't seem ladylike." Kathleen avoided looking at her. "They don't like hearing truths sometimes. Men are complicated. I'm sure you will find a husband, Hel. Your sisters did. You just have to be a little more quiet and demure. At least until the wedding."

Helene nodded as she forced herself up, trying not to let the tears fall. She didn't want to make her friend feel bad, especially since she had asked for her honest opinion. "Please excuse me. I need to freshen up."

"Oh, Hel, please don't leave. Who cares what gentlemen think? We are still years away from marriage. You do not have to decide your entire future now."

Helene gave her a brittle smile. "I'm afraid my parents won't give me years to decide."

The redhead had barely stepped out of the sitting room when she bumped headfirst into Zachary, who was dressed in a riding habit, seemingly returning from riding his horse. Even though he had his own bachelor quarters, he seemed to spend more time in his childhood home.

Helene blushed as she mumbled a hello. Had he heard how pathetic she had been? It was mortifying, how could she ever face him?

"And I thought you were one of those girls who didn't care about succeeding in the marriage mart." Zachary lips twitched in amusement, but never cruelty. He used his index finger and thumb to tilt her head forward so she was looking at him. "I must say I'm disappointed, Miss Hollis."

Helene's eyes burned with angry tears as she pulled back. "I thought we were addressing each other by our Christian names, Mr. Easton."

Zachary raised an eyebrow at her snappish tone, but at least he removed his fingers from her chin. She was too overwhelmed by what Kathleen had told her to be polite "We are, Helene."

Helene sniffed. "You do not care about succeeding in

the marriage mart because you are a gentleman from a good family. A handsome first son who will inherit everything from his father, who is well traveled, and attended one of the best universities in the country. Of course, you are not worried. You could get any wife you want."

"You think I'm handsome?"

Helene scowled. "My point is I do not have the same benefits you do."

"You're a daughter from the Hollis family. Your family was one of the first settlers from England to come to New York. One of your sisters married a wealthy Englishman and the other became a Darlington. I'm sure your prospects are not as dire as my sister makes them to be."

"That may be so, but because I'm the youngest, my dowry is not as big as it was for my sisters." Helene's shoulders slumped, surprised she was being so vocal with her best friend's older brother. "I'm also a redhead and I'm not as willowy as Audrina." With embarrassment, she used her arms to cover her large bosom which was starting to feel tight in her old dress.

Zachary shrugged. "The right man won't care about your dowry. You don't want a man who cannot provide for you or who is saddled with debts. Your red hair is lovely, much more vibrant than your sisters' black hair." He didn't mention the comment Helene had made about her figure and she was grateful for small miracles.

Her heart was pounding rapidly in her chest at the compliments Zachary gave her. He had always been polite to her, but she didn't think he would be this sweet. It was a pleasant surprise.

"Thank you, it's very kind of you to make me feel better."

"I'm not being kind, Helene, I am being truthful. Society places too much pressure on women to get married the minute they turn eighteen. It's unreasonable." He shook his head. "Please promise me you will not marry a fool, Helene. Believe me when I say it's better to be a spinster than to marry a man who cannot carry a conversation or someone whose brain is only there for a decorative purpose."

Helene giggled.

Zachary winked. "There is the smile I am used to seeing."

"If I am saddled with a foolish husband who cannot hold a conversation, I could always talk for the both of us."

"I'm sure that is every gentleman's fondest dream, to have his wife talk for hours." Zachary gently pinched her cheek as he had done when they had been children before he headed upstairs for a bath.

Helene's blue eyes followed him everywhere.

When Helene returned from Kathleen's house, she told the butler to inform her mother that she was ill and would not be joining them for dinner. She wasn't really ill, but she was full of pent up, nervous energy.

Once upstairs, with the help of her maid, she slipped into her nightgown, but she couldn't sleep. She kept thinking about Zachary, his cheeky smile, and the way he had pinched her cheek. It wasn't him being flirtatious, was it? No, he probably still saw her as his little sister's friend.

But it was the first time anyone had flirted with Helene. She had to admit she rather liked it. No wonder Corinne had put off marriage for so long. Flirting was quite fun.

She grabbed her pillow and stuffed it in between her legs. Helene didn't do this often because she didn't want to accidentally get caught by the servants, or worse, her mother. Only when she couldn't sleep.

Her bare quim rubbed against the soft pillow as Helene began straddling it. The pillow rubbed against the tight bundle of nerves hidden between her legs that she hardly touched because she felt embarrassed.

Usually, she dreamed about the men she read about in her romance novels that she discreetly hid in a box underneath her bed. This time, however, there was only one man who was plaguing her dreams. Zachary Easton.

She knew it was wrong to dream about her best friend's older brother, but she couldn't help it. He was handsome, young, rich, and available.

Her pale thighs gripped the pillow as her strokes became faster. Her breasts were bouncing inside her white nightgown as her fingers rubbed her clit. She could feel the pillow becoming soaked with her juices beneath her and she would have to let it dry out before the maids started asking questions.

She imagined Zachary winking at her before he pulled her in for a kiss, Zachary stroking the sensitive part of her upper breasts while she was tightly corseted, Zachary gripping the back of each thigh while he—

A loud moan escaped her lips. Usually, she was very careful in containing any unusual sounds, but this time she lost control of the situation as she let the pleasure ride her body. Her trembling legs gave up on her as she fell headfirst into the pillows.

There was a knock on the door seconds later. "Uh, Miss Hollis, are you all right?"

"Yes, I'm sorry, I had a leg cramp. You are dismissed, thank you."

Helene breathed a sigh of relief when she heard the maid walk away. It had been a very long day indeed.

Chapter 3

I t was Kathleen's eighteenth birthday, and since the poor thing was so shy and hated being the center of attention, her father had organized an early afternoon garden party instead. Kathleen insisted it was very fashionable and done in Paris all the time, but Helene could tell she was relieved she was not expected to be the guest of honor at a large ball.

Her father, however, had invited more people than Kathleen had anticipated and the Eastons' small garden was now crawling with a least three dozen people, which was making poor Kat break out in hives.

Helene alternated between comforting her friend by slipping her glasses of champagne to calm her nerves and looking at prospective husbands so her mother didn't marry her off to a wealthy old man who could be her father.

Blue eyes looked around her surroundings, focusing on the young men she knew who were single and could be prospective husbands. There was Mr. Eldridge, but his laugh was a bit obnoxious, then there was Mr. Simon, but rumors were he had gambled away his fortune and was looking for a rich heiress. There was also Mr. Conway, but he was a widower and he still looked sad at the loss of his wife.

Growing bored and overheated, she quickly went inside to relieve herself after drinking too many glasses of champagne and to make sure her unruly red hair still looked halfway decent. The heat always made her hair become an embarrassing mess.

After making sure it looked acceptable and she had emptied her bladder, she made her way back outside to continue her husband hunting endeavors. Helene stopped when she heard loud laughter coming from the Eastons' downstairs library where the gentlemen went to rest or for private conversation.

Even with her full skirts, Helene managed to hide between one of the Greek statues to peek inside the library without anyone seeing her. From what she could see, there were about fifteen gentlemen dressed in their best afternoon clothes in various stages of intoxication which Helene always found fascinating.

She quickly saw Zachary nursing a glass of whisky, a lazy expression on his face as the men grew rowdy around him.

"How's married life treating you, Clifford?"

Mr. Clifford had recently married Miss Huntington.

Helene couldn't see Mr. Clifford's face, but she could practically hear the glee in his voice. "She was as tight as new violin strings, gentlemen. I don't believe my Gemma could do more than lie down the next day."

Loud laughter erupted from the gentlemen as some of them patted Mr. Clifford's back. Helene knew she should leave. It was rude to listen to others' conversations, not to mention this was not the type of conversation an unmarried lady should overhear. But it was like Helene's feet were glued to the floor.

The conversation continued about poor Gemma and Mr. Clifford's wedding night. Now she knew why Gemma had been so miserable and refused to attend social events.

"Easton, are you bedding Jane? How is the best whore in all of New York?"

Helene gasped, but thankfully the men's loud laughter prevented her from being overheard. She didn't know why she was so surprised. Lots of unmarried men slept with prostitutes, even married ones. Sometimes they even produced bastard children which her mother had hinted happened more often than not.

Zachary still had the bored expression on his face. "I have not bedded Jane in months; she has bored me beyond repair. I finally decided to let her services go."

"You could borrow my Judith once I am done with her," Mr. Willis offered, his double chin jiggling. "She knows how to make your troubles disappear."

A younger man with wheat-blond hair whacked his shoulder. "I've seen his Judith, Easton. You're not missing much. The girl is as scrawny as a weed. Maybe you should share some of your food with her instead of hogging it all."

Mr. Willis reddened.

"I am not interested in bedding a woman currently," Zachary answered coolly.

"Don't tell me you are planning to marry?"

"All men who are planning on marrying always try to behave like saints before they wed. It never lasts, especially after they wed and the babies come."

"No marriage for me. I am looking for a husband for my little sister, which will not be any of you fools."

The room exploded in laughter. The blond man placed

a hand on Zachary's shoulder. "You won't last long, Easton. Believe me, all men crave the pleasure of the female flesh."

Zachary didn't answer; instead, he motioned for Mr. Willis to give him a cigar, obviously bored of the conversation already.

Helene hurried away from the library before the men came out, and found herself back in the garden. The words *the pleasure of the female flesh* kept ringing in her ear. Her mother had always compared men to animals. Maybe she had not been wrong after all.

The redhead thought back to her older sister, Corinne. Before she had been forced to marry her Englishman, she had been quite a popular girl, with men tripping over themselves to win her approval. She had even been proposed to six times before she married.

Corinne was beautiful, which was the reason why she had been so successful, but she had also been knowledgeable about pleasuring men. If Helene learned to pleasure men with her own body then perhaps she would have the opportunity to have half as many proposals as Corinne.

She didn't know if any relationship she had would turn to love, but at least she would marry a man of her own choosing instead of one her parents chose for her.

For the first time all day, Helene finally smiled.

Chapter 4

As a bachelor, Zachary did not share the same residence with his father and Kathleen. Instead, he lived in a modest brownstone painted a dark, rust color which reminded Helene of cinnamon. Despite its elegance, Helene couldn't help but notice that it looked a bit sad due to lack of movement and servants.

Though Helene guessed it made things better that he lived on such a lonely street because it meant less people would notice that Helene Hollis, the unmarried daughter of the Hollis family, was visiting an unwed bachelor in the middle of the night in the future.

Still, one couldn't be too careful and Helene had dressed the part to make herself as undetectable as possible. She was in a thick mourning gown she hadn't worn in three years which made it tight around the bosom and hips. Her slender, pale hands were covered in thick, black gloves, and her unruly red hair was tucked underneath a wide, black hat.

A shiver ran down her back. She wondered if this was even a good idea in the first place. But who else could she turn to? Kathleen was just as clueless as she and she couldn't ask her mother to help her with this endeavor. The old woman would probably faint. She wished Corinne were here.

Corinne had had sexual relationships with several men before she was forced to marry Nicholas when she was caught. If anyone would be able to teach her how to please a man and get the husband of her choosing, it would be her. But it took so long to receive letters from England, not to mention her sister could sometimes be mean, and she didn't want to look like a complete fool.

Helene needed to get married and this was her only chance. Zachary was a well-traveled man, not to mention the only man outside of her family she was semi-close to. She knew Zachary wouldn't be spreading harmful gossip around about the type of women Helene was.

She took a deep breath before knocking on the door.

An elderly butler answered. He raised his bushy eyebrows in surprise, obviously not used to receiving female guests. Even when they were dressed like a widow. The butler cleared his throat. "Good morning, ma'am. How can I help you?"

"Good morning, I came to see Mr. Easton. Is he in?"

"Do you have a calling card?"

"Not with me. You can tell him it is Kathleen Easton's friend calling for him."

It was clear the butler wanted to ask her more but didn't want to pressure a woman. He led her to the small sitting room which looked like no one spent time in it, based on how stiff everything looked. When the butler asked if she wanted tea, she refused. The less people knew that she was here, the better.

While the butler went to search for the master of the house, Helene looked around the sitting room. It was quite obvious a man had decorated it instead of a woman. The room was decorated in dark colors instead of the rich, vibrant colors women like her mother preferred. There wasn't a single flower decoration in the room.

Instead, the only decorations happened to be an ancient wooden clock, the head of a buck at the center above the stone fireplace with its eyes frozen in fear, and a long, wooden cane below the buck, no doubt once belonging to the Easton siblings' grandfather.

Helene shuddered. No wonder unmarried ladies weren't allowed in bachelor's homes. It was not pleasant.

Her thoughts about how she could decorate Zachary's house if she was the lady of the house were interrupted when Zachary stormed into the room, pushing the door even more open. Helene could see the front door and the confused butler quite clearly from her stance.

It was clear Zachary had just finished taking a bath when he had come downstairs because his clothes, while clean, were rumpled and his glossy brown hair was stuck to his forehead.

He didn't relax when he saw her, in fact, he kept looking at her as if she were a burglar. His face was tense and he hadn't smiled once since he'd entered the room.

Helene frowned. This was not what she had been expecting.

Zachary had always been friendly to her, so why the sudden change? He was looking at her as if she were the enemy. It was not a pleasant sensation. Had she done something to offend him?

"What are you doing here, Miss Hollis?" he asked rudely as he looked around the room and then over his shoulder to make sure his butler was still facing the main door. "Are you hurt? Is there something wrong with Kathleen?"

"No, she's fine, and I'm fine." Helene was starting to regret coming here in the first place. She smoothed down her black skirt as she stood up. "I wanted to speak to you."

"You could have done that when you visited Kathleen the other day or I could have called on you at your home," he argued coldly.

Helene laughed nervously. He was making her feel like a naughty little girl. "We wouldn't have had complete privacy. My mother or your sister would have gotten suspicious or started fussing."

He didn't argue. "Still, it's highly improper for an unmarried young woman to visit a bachelor's home, especially if they are not related. If anyone were to recognize you, even in your ridiculous mourning clothes, both of our reputations would be ruined. Yours more than mine, I'm afraid, Miss Hollis."

Helene looked hurt. "Miss Hollis? What happened to Helene? And I thought you didn't care about what other people said."

"I don't, but my father expects me to stay in New York to take over the family business. New York is a small town, the people are small-minded. I would rather not burn any bridges before I begin." He stood by the doorway. "I must insist you leave, Miss Hollis."

Helene widened her blue eyes like an injured puppy. She hated doing this to manipulate people, but she only used it as a last resort. "Please, Zachary. Just give me five minutes of your time. I just wanted to have a private conversation. I didn't mean any disrespect, I swear."

Zachary hesitated, but eventually, he groaned and agreed. He closed the sitting room doors, much to his butler's disapproval by the way his eyes grew wide.

The man of the house sat in the chair across from her, placing a hand on his chin as he stared at her as if she were an interesting specimen, with a hint of irritation crossing his handsome features. He really looked much better when he was smiling. "Speak, young lady, before my butler faints from this entire event alone."

Helene cleared her throat as she sat up with a confident smile on her face. "You know my older sister, Corinne, do you not? You two are the same age."

"Unfortunately," he agreed with no trace of warmth. Many people did not like Corinne. Women, because she had often slept with their husbands or beaus. Men, because they had either been rejected by her or she was black-mailing them in some way. Zachary did not like Corinne because she was snobbish.

"Well, you do remember that my sister was very popular before she married—"

"Before she was forced to marry, yes. What are you trying to say, Helene?"

Helene bit her pinky nail, trying to figure out how to best bring this conversation to light. "Do you remember why she was popular and had so many marriage proposals even though she was past marriable age?"

Zachary reddened as Helene looked on with amuse-ment. It was cute seeing a man blush. "I cannot say in front of a lady."

"She's my sister, Zachary. I knew what she was doing behind closed doors even before I came out. Cor was never discreet with me and Audrina when it came to her love life."

Zachary muttered something under his breath before he gave her an irritated look. "What does your sister have to do with our conversation?"

"Well, she and Audrina are in England now," she continued nervously. "You must be aware that my prospects are not as plentiful as theirs, but I do want to be married, even if you look down at the idea. I have decided the best thing to do to get my pick of suitors is to be like Corinne."

"Unlikeable? Selfish? Vain?"

She ignored him. "An expert in the marriage bed, before marriage. That is the way she was." Her cheeks pinkened. "However, since I have no one to teach me and it takes so long to receive English post, I was hoping you could teach me instead, the tricks I need to learn to properly catch a husband."

Zachary looked furious; his entire face was red though she was not sure the exact reason for it. "You want me to teach you, an unmarried virgin, how to seduce men to get them to propose?"

Helene nodded, trying not to look too eager. "I must insist on a man's opinion. I will not share a bed with them like Cor did. I want to remain a virgin until marriage to avoid a baby, but Corinne told me and Audrina there are other ways to pleasure men with your hands and mouth."

"You are well prepared, Hel. Did you ever stop to think that the men you're hopelessly trying to seduce will just use you as their plaything and bolt?"

"Corinne used to blackmail men to prevent them from sharing the fact that she made love to them."

"There are other ways around it. Men talk and gossip just as much as women do. You could be called a redheaded Jezebel, or worse. Your family's reputation might never recover. They are still talking about your sister's affair with the Englishman."

"I'd rather be called a whore than a spinster!" Helene snapped, finally showing her true reaction. She stood up. Coming here was a mistake. She had thought this would be a fun journey on her quest to get married. She hadn't expected Zachary to insult her and treat her like a hopeless, naïve little girl. She knew the consequences, but unfortunately for her, she didn't have the option to be choosy, something Zachary would never understand. "I thought you would be able to help me. Apparently, I was wrong. I am truly sorry for bothering you, Mr. Easton. Perhaps I can find another gentleman to assist me on my quest. I wouldn't want to destroy your precious reputation that you do care about, after all."

Before she could open the door of the sitting room, she felt Zachary grip her arm and tug her back into the center of the room. Helene squirmed away, but he was much stronger. She really was in no state of mind to hear a lecture about the importance of womanly virtue. Now that Zachary had ruined her plans, she had to find another gentleman who was willing to help her with her plan.

Her thoughts were interrupted when she found herself placed over his lap. She blinked. What was he trying to do? Lying over a man's lap was never comfortable, but especially so while wearing this heavy mourning dress.

Before Helene could ask him what he was doing, she felt his large hand slap down against her upturned rear. The redhead shrieked at the impact. Zachary responded by landing an equally hard slap against her other cheek, leaving behind a terrible sting.

It finally occurred to her that Zachary was spanking her! She had never been spanked on her rear end before. When she had been a little girl, her nannies had often just slapped the back of her hands or pinched her if she misbehaved. She knew her sister, Audrina, got spanked by her husband because she had overheard her sister being spanked earlier in the year.

She had thought Zachary was different than Dominic. Apparently, she was quite wrong.

The slaps continued to rain down on her rear end,

which caused her bottom to grow hotter. She wouldn't be surprised if it had swelled up to twice its size. Helene tried squirming away from him, but Zachary was holding her by the hips firmly which made even attempting to run away impossible.

Tears stung her eyes as her cheeks kept bouncing lewdly against his hard palm. The slaps echoed loudly in the sitting room. She wouldn't be surprised if Zachary's servants were whispering about how Miss Hollis was getting her bottom roasted.

"Please stop, I'm sorry." Helene wasn't sure what she was apologizing for exactly. She just knew she wanted the spanking to stop.

The tears fell down her cheeks as Zachary continued peppering her bottom, making sure he covered every inch of her bottom and the backs of her thighs. She was just grateful he hadn't pulled up her skirts and given her a proper spanking.

Zachary landed one last, loud smack in the center on her plump cheeks which caused her to yelp. He finally let her go and she stood up immediately, eager to get away from him. Her hands clutched her poor, sore bottom cheeks as she began rubbing them, trying to soothe away the pain.

Helene couldn't even bear to look at him, she felt too embarrassed because she'd been punished. Zachary had made her feel like a spoiled little brat. Zachary did not offer comfort or apologies even when he saw her bouncing around his sitting room trying to soothe her sore rear end.

"Get out, Miss Hollis," he hissed at her cruelly. "And don't come back, especially with that ridiculous request."

Helene didn't have to be told twice. She raced out of the room like a bat straight out of hell, even ignoring the butler's look of pity as he asked if he should halt a rented carriage to take her home.

The young woman had used her pin money to take a rented carriage to Zachary's home, but the idea of sitting on a sore bottom sounded like a complete nightmare. Instead, she ran like her life depended on it. Helene was surprised she didn't trip over her skirts.

She managed to calm down somewhat when she finally made it home. She dried her tears with the backs of her hands before she made her way down to the servant's entrance. She couldn't go through the front entrance dressed like this.

Thankfully, the servants were too busy preparing dinner that they didn't notice the young girl in black making her way up the stairs. Thank goodness Mother had a meeting with one of her many charity committees and Father was probably in the gentleman's club drinking with his friends or playing a game of cards.

It was moments like this, Helene desperately wished she had her sisters with her. They would make her feel better and comfort her about being spanked by her best friend's brother. The mourning gown was hard to get rid of, but she managed to remove it until she was just in her chemise and drawers. She would have to sleep naked tonight; she wouldn't be able to stand anything on her scorching rear end.

Gingerly, she raised her chemise and turned around to inspect her spanked bottom in the mirror Mother had given to her from Paris for her seventeenth birthday. A gasp escaped her lips when she saw her spanked bottom.

Her usually pale cheeks were bright red, as vibrant as her own hair. The punished skin was covered in Zachary's large handprints and she was surprised how much damage he'd managed to inflict when he'd spanked her over her skirts. She could hardly believe she had Zachary's marks on her.

Helene's womanhood throbbed as she felt her nectar pooling between her legs like it often did when she was humping her pillow in the middle of the night. She shook her head as she pressed a hand against a welt on her lower cheek. She should have slapped him for being so cruel. It was the least he deserved.

If he didn't approve, he should have just said no, there was no need to punish her. Her hands touched her poor cheeks trying to rub away the pain but touching them only inflicted more pain.

A sniff escaped from her as she dropped down her chemise. She wouldn't be able to sit for the next few days, all thanks to Zachary.

Miles away in Zachary Easton's bachelor home, Zachary was nursing a scotch after dismissing the butler and the rest of his servants for the evening. Zachary was drunk. Very drunk. To the point he couldn't remember how much he had drunk. He needed to be careful or he would vomit all over the Persian carpets.

His only thought for the past two hours was Helene Hollis. He couldn't help but think back to her tear-stained face, the way her lower lip had trembled adorably, and most of all, the way her bottom had bounced against his hand repeatedly as he had spanked her.

Helene's bottom had felt plump and soft, exactly as a woman's body should be. He was glad she had been too busy squirming that she hadn't noticed his erection pressing against her lower belly.

Zachary hadn't planned to spank her, but he had

grown furious when she had barged into his bachelor home and even more so when she asked him to help her seduce men. If someone would have asked him, he would have said all three Hollis girls deserved a good spanking for being so flighty.

Thankfully, the two older women had husbands, but it meant he had to deal with the younger one. He knew Helene was stubborn, and if he didn't agree to her stupid plan, she would go to someone else.

Zachary couldn't have that. He supposed he should apologize first.

Chapter 5

Zachary hated wearing evening clothes because of how stiff and uncomfortable they were. Unfortunately, they were a necessity in New York city ballrooms. He had been here for two hours, fake smiling and pretending to hear dull conversations with young men his age who had nothing of substance to speak about.

Zachary did not have friends. He preferred to spend time with himself; even his sister thought it was odd he preferred the quiet. Kathleen was on the ladies' side of the ballroom where young girls waited for young men to ask them to dance while the matrons looked on suspiciously.

He had asked his sister several times if Helene Hollis would be attending. Kathleen had given him a funny look before she had said yes. He hoped she would. He did not want to visit the Hollis home; her mother was insufferable and he didn't want Mr. Hollis to think he was courting their daughter.

Thirty more minutes, he told himself as he sipped on his drink, trying his best not to get drunk. *If she's not here by then,*

I'll leave. I have better things to do than spend my night in a ballroom.

As if summoning her, Mrs. Hollis and Helene stepped inside the ballroom. Mr. Hollis rarely attended these type of events. Helene was dressed in a cream and dark pink dress with overly puffed sleeves. Her beautiful red hair was arranged in an elegant bun at the nape of her neck and covered with tiny pink flowers.

The two women greeted their hosts for the evening. As soon as Helene noticed Zachary's presence, she gave a tiny scowl in his direction so her mother didn't see.

Zachary's lip twitched in amusement. She was rather adorable when she wasn't fussing with herself about what was proper. He was suddenly angry at all the men who had rejected Helene. She was far more interesting than half of the ladies here tonight and her red hair suited her perfectly.

Helene was about to hide with the rest of the ladies, but Zachary managed to stop her by getting in front of her, startling both mother and daughter. "Good evening, Mrs. Hollis, Miss Hollis, both of you look lovely this evening. Miss Hollis, would you grant me the honor of dancing with me?"

Helene pursed her lips, obviously wanting to reject him, but not wanting to be seen as rude. She had just gotten here so she couldn't pretend to be tired. It worked out perfectly. "Yes, Mr. Easton, I gladly accept."

He grinned in satisfaction while Mrs. Hollis gave him a suspicious look. It was fun teasing his younger sister, but he hadn't thought it would be fun to tease her best friend too. Zachary offered his hand towards the young woman and she took it reluctantly as he led her to the center of the dance floor before the music began.

Helene blushed when she found herself in the middle

of the dance floor, not used to being the center of attention. She looked at him with wide eyes as if begging him to move, but he shook his head, giving her a firm, "No." Then he cocked his head to the side. "You belong in the center of the dance floor, Miss Hollis. I won't hear any argument from you."

Helene narrowed her eyes angrily, and he was almost sure she wanted to slap him. He liked this new side of her. She was a spitfire when it was only the two of them. It made Zachary proud he was able to bring out a different side of her.

The music began and Zachary bowed in her direction while Helene curtsied, giving him a delicious view of those full, pale breasts that were begging for his attention. His cock stirred in his pants. It had been too long since he had been with a woman. He had almost forgotten what it was like. Helene's skin, even through her pale pink gloves, felt warm and inviting,

Helene stopped frowning at him and instead just focused on the dance. She really was an excellent dancer and he didn't have to worry about stepped-on toes or clumsy movements when he was with her. If she wasn't a lady, she could have had a career on stage, especially with her vibrant hair.

"How's your bottom?" he asked casually once he grew tired of her silent treatment.

Helene blushed bright red as she looked around, afraid someone else had heard. "Zachary! It's inappropriate!" She lowered her voice. "Someone could hear."

He leaned forward, whispering in her ear, "The music is too loud, Miss Hollis. No one will be the wiser. Now, I will ask again, how is your bottom? Not sore, I hope."

It had been three days since she had forced her way inside his house.

Helene refused to answer.

Her stubbornness wasn't exactly adorable, but he had a way of making her talk. "Answer me, Helene, or you will leave me no choice but to inspect for myself."

A gasp escaped her lips, her eyes widening. "You wouldn't." Poor thing was so embarrassed.

"Do you really want to test that fact, Miss Hollis?"

Helene shook her head, her face becoming as red as her hair. "I'm still a little sore, but the color has gone away, mostly."

"Poor pet." He clicked his tongue sympathetically. "I should have been kinder to you. I behaved inappropriately last time. I should have comforted you and offered you some salve for you posterior."

Zachary twirled Helene around. "You're apologizing for not comforting me, not for spanking me?"

"No, you deserved that spanking. You know the rules as well as I. You ran a great risk barging into my home and then demanding I teach you unladylike things. I needed to teach you a lesson your bottom wouldn't forget."

"You shouldn't have spanked me, I'm not a child," she hissed in return.

"Spanking has nothing to do with age. If a woman does something which warrants a spanking, she should be spanked. I see your father has not disciplined you, and your sisters have given you bad advice. If your father won't correct you, then I will."

Helene scowled at him, but there was still some blush coating her cheeks.

"So, you would spank me again?"

"Yes, if the situation warrants it."

The redhead pursed her lips as if she didn't agree. She kept looking at him as if wondering if he was fibbing, but he wasn't. He wasn't a stranger to spanking women in bed to increase their pleasure, but when he had spanked Helene, it had been the first time he had done it to discipline someone.

Zachary hadn't regretted it. If someone needed a spanking, it was the redheaded little miss. "I wanted to talk to you about your offer, Helene, before the song ends."

Helene perked up, suddenly interested. "Yes?"

"I am willing to be your teacher on one condition."

"Which is?"

"I choose your husband for you. You are a young girl with your head in the clouds. You don't understand how men think."

Helene looked offended, but when she saw Zachary wasn't backing out, she reluctantly agreed. "Fine. But he must have money and come from a good family. My family won't accept anything else. You must talk me up to the men at your gentlemen's club or wherever you spend your time. Let them know I am available; that is the perfect way to catch a husband. Tiffany Gold gave me that very sound advice."

Zachary snorted but nodded. "Now, for the lessons you mentioned, you do not have to go to bed with these men to prove your point. You are not Corinne Hollis, thank heavens. A light flirtation will get men interested in you to propose marriage."

Helene seemed to consider this before she slowly nodded. "Fine. I will not entertain men like my sister did, but I still expect you to teach me about how I should act in the marriage bed. Tricks and such." She was speaking of herself as if she were to be a trained puppy. "I do not want to go to bed a silly virgin."

"You're eighteen years old, you are supposed to be a silly virgin," he hissed at her as, much to his chagrin, he grew red at the prospect of deflowering Helene Hollis.

"How are you going to explain to your husband that you're not a maiden?"

Helene shrugged. "Let me worry about him. I am not a complete fool." She raised her chin proudly like a young queen. "So, you will accept my offer if I let you choose my husband?"

He narrowed his eyes, trying to intimidate her. It wasn't working, "Fine, but don't cry when you regret giving up your maidenhood."

"I won't," she replied haughtily. "When do we start?"

The song ended as Zachary bowed to her, and Helene curtsied. "Tomorrow afternoon around four, before dinner, when you won't be missed. Come in disguise," he ordered firmly. The last thing they needed was a gossipy servant or old biddy to spread the rumor that Zachary Easton and Helene Hollis were having an affair. "Come through the servants' entrance in the back. The servants should be having their tea by then and we won't be disturbed. Meet me in my bedroom, upstairs, third door to your left. We will conduct our training for an hour and then you'll go home. If either of us becomes uncomfortable with the situation, we will break it off. If you barge into my home unannounced like you did earlier this week, I will blister your bottom until sitting becomes just a memory. Understood?"

Helene nodded eagerly.

"Hel, no one can find out about this. Not your sisters and especially not my sister."

The girl nodded. Zachary suddenly felt exhausted. He was going to end up in Hell for even entertaining little Helene Hollis. He felt his erection grow in his trousers at the prospect of kissing her creamy skin. He needed to get out of here now.

"Um, pardon me for interrupting, but, Miss Hollis,

may I have this next dance?" A young man around Helene's age bowed then offered his hand, his eyes never leaving Zachary, as if he was afraid Zachary was going to punch him. Coward.

Helene looked pleased and didn't bother glancing at Zachary again, as if he were an old shoe. "I would be delighted, Mr. Ashton. Thank you for the dance, Mr. Easton."

Zachary watched as Helene went to dance with the idiot with the two left feet. He felt something bubbling inside his chest. He wasn't sure what it was, but it was not pleasant.

The next morning, Zachary felt distracted and anxious, like he wanted to jump out the window. He had been trying to read *Hamlet* for the past hour with little success. He wondered how he would explain to his servants if Helene was caught.

With his luck, news would spread by this afternoon and he would find himself married on Sunday to protect both of their reputations. Zachary did not want to get married, especially not to Helene. She was still practically in the schoolhouse. No, once Zachary married, it would be to a well-bred young lady around his age who wasn't so delusional.

Zachary heard a racket coming from outside before a small figure stormed inside his bedroom dressed in a black and white maid's uniform with their red hair tucked in a white cap. Helene.

Helene looked over her shoulder, relieved she had not been seen before she turned back to Zachary with a proud look on her face. "I made it."

"So, you did. What's with all the racket?"

"I stumbled on the upper steps. I saw your butler

heading towards the front entrance," she confessed, her cheeks flushed.

Zachary's lip twitched. The girl could be amusing, he would give her that.

"What are you wearing?"

Helene's face fell. "You told me to come in costume. I thought this was better than my widow costume." The maid uniform was too baggy on her, hiding her curves, but he had to admit it did the job.

Zachary nodded as he studied her, trying to make sense of how he would start his "lesson" even though his awakening cock probably had an idea or two. "We should get started, we don't have much time. I will ask you again, are you sure you want me to take your virginity? It could provide problems later on."

She nodded. "I'll manage. Teach me."

Zachary was not usually a nervous man, but when he looked at the slight girl in front of him, he had to be honest, he felt like running in the opposite direction. He had seen Helene playing with dolls and running around with bows in her hair, and now he was supposed to take her virginity?

Helene must have noticed his anxiety because her lips curled into a mischievous grin. "My, Mr. Easton, are you feeling nervous? I thought you were an experienced man. Perhaps I picked the wrong teacher after all."

"Be quiet, Helene." Even though his tone was gruff, his hands trembled as he tried to unbutton the black buttons of her maid's dress. When she saw him struggling, she rolled her eyes and unbuttoned them herself, until the gown was wrapped around her ankles.

Zachary held his breath when he saw Helene only dressed in a thin, white chemise. No drawers, corset, or other annoying female frivolity in sight. He took in her round, pale thighs and the pink nipples which were visible through the outline of the thin fabric.

Helene let out a frustrated sigh when she saw he had not moved. Her fingers removed the chemise, giving Zachary a rare view of her nakedness. His jaw went slack and she was surprised he was not drooling over the floor.

Helene Hollis was perfection from head to toe and Zachary wasn't sure if he had seen a more beautiful woman. He suddenly wanted to throttle everyone who tried to convince Helene that she wasn't as beautiful as her sisters. He thought she was the most beautiful girl of all.

Some of the bravado was gone as a pink flush erupted across her face and neck. She squirmed but never once tried to shield herself, and he was proud of that fact. Her beauty shouldn't be hidden. There was a soft patch of vibrant red hair between her legs.

Zachary took a step forward to her and gently cupped one of her breasts. He expected her to turn away, but she didn't. His thumb grazed her pink nipple lightly. She let out a small cry, caught off guard about how good it felt.

Zachary couldn't help but smirk. Oh, yes, he was going to have a lot of fun with her. "Not feeling so brave right now, Hel, are you?" He squeezed her breast as his other hand cupped a small, round buttock.

Helene glared at him like a proud kitten. "I wasn't the one who was scared to take his clothes off."

His pride was wounded a bit at her words and he decided on payback. Zachary tipped her chin forward so they were facing each other, then he kissed her. His kiss was dominating and strong, making her eat her words.

Helene returned the kiss eagerly, her hand touching the back of his neck. She pulled back, pleasantly pleased, her big doe eyes looking at him with lust.

Zachary's cock felt like it was going to break and it was

all the redheaded devil's fault. Who knew the little minx was so passionate?

Every part of Zachary was screaming that this was a mistake, that he should stop right now before he bitterly regretted it, but his manhood had a mind of its own. Gone, were all his clothes, until he was just as naked as Miss Hollis.

Her eyes widened adorably as she stared at him, looking as if she was about to faint. It occurred to Zachary that he was the first man whom she had seen naked and he was the only one who had seen her beautiful, curvy figure. Zachary couldn't help but feel proud of the fact even though if he said it out loud, Helene would probably think he was hopelessly vain.

The idea of another man seeing her naked, even if said man was her husband, irked him for some reason even though it was what she was promised.

Helene gulped, her baby blue eyes never steering away from his cock. It twitched with need, and Helene jumped, hitting her back against the bookshelf.

Zachary chuckled, enjoying the way her bosom fell with her jump. "Careful, it won't bite."

Helene swallowed, still staring at his manhood as if it were covered in thorns. "I don't think it will fit."

"Don't be silly. I've been with women smaller than you."

Helene glared at him, her cheeks flushing with a mixture of rage and embarrassment. "But I've never lain with anyone."

Zachary bit his tongue. He knew nothing about dealing with fussy females other than his sister, but he had a feeling mentioning his past with other women might not be ideal. Maybe he should just stop talking altogether.

"I'll be gentle." He took a step forward, while Helene

took a step backward. He suddenly fantasized about chasing her around his bedroom naked so he could watch every part of her delightful body bounce. "Helene, you were enjoying yourself before. Now come here. I promise I will not hurt you."

Helene hesitated before she reluctantly made her way towards him like a scared fawn. "Kiss me," he ordered firmly.

"What?"

"Kiss me."

Helene hesitated before she did as she was told. While she was distracted with the kiss, Zachary parted her plump thighs, giving him access to the charms hidden under her red curls.

Helene squeaked when she felt his fingers rub against her folds. When she tried to pull away, he placed one hand on her buttocks, squeezing them. Helene blushed but didn't move. It looked like she was anticipating his next move.

His fingers started rubbing against her lower lips until he felt the wetness pool around them. Every once in a while, he would brush his thumb against her clit which was still safely hidden in its hood.

Helene would then adorably let out a small gasp of need and wiggle her hips. It wouldn't be hard to make her scream his name. It was a shame they had to be relatively quiet for the servants downstairs, not that any of them would dare question him if they heard girlish screams.

Once he was sure she was wet enough, the master of the house dipped one finger into her sweet love lips. Helene jumped but didn't pull away as he pumped one finger into her, stretching her as much as he could, but she was unbearably tight.

A whimper escaped her lips as Helene stared at him with watery eyes as if she were afraid he was going to kill her. "Relax," he murmured as he kissed her lower lip gently. "I would never hurt you, you know that, Hel. I'm going to try to make your first time as pleasant as possible. Do you trust me?"

Helene nodded as he murmured sweet nothings into her ear. This was a mistake, what was Zachary Easton doing with a proper, well-bred virgin? But it was too late to back away now.

When he noticed she had relaxed a bit, he started kissing her neck before trailing down to those sweet, full breasts he wanted to bury himself in. His teeth started nibbling on the sensitive flesh, scraping against her quickly hardening nipples.

A whimper filled with pleasure escaped from her as she arched herself forward, their hips touching. She was so soft, he was afraid he would break her. His erection was now rubbing against her lower belly, covering it with the wetness from the tip of his cock.

Zachary entered a second finger inside her and then a third, stretching her as much as he could to prepare her for him. Helene didn't seem to mind this time because he was still playing with her breasts.

He tore his lips away from her breasts to circle her engorged clit a few times until he was sure she was wet enough for him. Helene, by this point, was panting, her skin flushed, and a wet mess between her legs.

She was looking at him, her blue eyes filled with desire that most of New York society would deem unladylike, but that he thought made her look like a goddess. He needed to have her now.

Zachary picked her up like a new bride as he took her to his bed. He lay down on the large, four-poster bed and placed her on top of him until she was straddling his belly, his manhood now poking the back of her buttocks.

"What are you doing?" she asked, confused. "Aren't I supposed to be lying on my back?"

He chuckled. "There isn't some kind of rule book, Hel. This is better for your first time. You will be able to control the speed of our lovemaking."

Helene looked a bit confused, but she nodded anyway.

"Now, listen carefully, I am going to grip you by your hips and place you down on my cock." Helene winced when he said the word "cock". "It will be painful since this is your first time, but try not to squirm. Otherwise, you will make it worse on yourself. Understood?"

She nodded, briefly looking at the door as if thinking about running away.

"Everything will be fine, Hel." He cupped her cheek in his hand. "You just have to trust me. I would never hurt you."

Helene kept a brave smile on her face as Zachary gripped her hips. He could easily lift her up despite her obvious concerns. Her bottom and thighs dangled over his body. Many men went extremely slow with their wives on their wedding night, but Zachary thought the best way to get rid of the pesky piece of hidden flesh was to do it as quickly as possible.

He had barely lifted Helene up when he then plopped her down on his hardened erection. Helene yelped and tried to squirm away at the sudden pain, but Zachary didn't let her; instead, he positioned himself until every inch was buried inside her sweet cunt.

Tears stung Helene's eyes as blood covered the mushroom head of his manhood. "It's all over now, sweetheart," he cooed as he started rubbing her clit so she could feel pleasure instead of all the pain. "Just focus on enjoying now. Rotate your hips for me, darling. I promise it will feel better now."

Despite the uncomfortableness, Helene did as she was told. She moved her sweet little hips to the rhythm of his gentle thrusts while he continued rubbing her clit, focusing on the center of it which drove women insane with lust.

The tears of pain soon disappeared from Helene's face, and instead, they were replaced with whimpers of satisfaction as they continued with their lovemaking, their bodies becoming one. Her breasts gently bounced while he squeezed one buttock.

His strokes became faster while he alternated between pinching Helene's bundle of nerves and caressing it lovingly. She was close to reaching that level of satisfaction all women long for.

A lovely scream erupted from Helene's lips as she reached her pleasure. It was the sweetest sound he had ever heard. Zachary wished he could hear it over and over again. The look Helene gave him was priceless; it was like she was looking at him in a different light.

Zachary was almost ready to reach his own pleasure, but he forced himself to contain his need. The last thing he needed was to get Helene pregnant. It would be too cruel on both Helene and the child to have an unexpected pregnancy.

Instead, he pressed his hands around her hips, raised her up slightly, and covered the nearby throw pillow with his seed instead of her cunt like his body begged him to do.

She stumbled forward, her legs too shaky to contain herself upright anymore. Her breasts were pressed on his face. His tongue poked out of his mouth, licking her nipple, and causing her to giggle.

He waited for the guilt or the cries of anguish because Helene had willingly lost her virginity to the man who would never marry her. But it never came. In fact, she looked almost content, as if she had gotten a horrible procedure out of the way. Zachary didn't know if he should be offended or not.

Zachary was disappointed when her bosom disappeared from his face. "It wasn't as bad as I had been expecting. Thank you."

He cleared his throat. "You're welcome." He sat up slowly, pressing his hand gently on her hip. Helene winced. "Sorry." She was probably still sore.

"Why did you pull away suddenly?" she asked him with a flushed face.

He pointed to the cum on the pillow. Zachary would have to clean it before the maids came to tidy up. They did not need to see that. "If I fill you with my seed, there is a good chance I could get you pregnant. I don't want to risk it. I will never fill you with my seed, I promise, Helene."

Helene nodded. He'd expected her to look relieved, but dare he say, she almost looked disappointed. Maybe Helene had more dirty thoughts than Zachary had imagined.

His eyes drifted towards her lower half. Her slit and inner thighs were covered with dried blood, and the tip of his cock was slightly pink, covered with her virginal blood.

Helene was looking up at him like a shy fawn. She was too shy and sweet for her own good. There was a reason why his old roommate at Harvard told him to never sleep with a virgin who wasn't his wife. They got too attached. Now, Zachary wished he had listened to him.

Zachary cleared his throat as he picked up a clean washcloth and wet it with water from the nearby pitcher in the corner of his bedroom where his valet usually shaved him. "Spread your legs."

Helene did as she was told, giving him a look at her

quim which was now covered with her virginal blood. He gently dabbed at the affected area with the washcloth, trying to be as gentle as possible, but the young woman still winced.

"Does it hurt? Are you sure? Be honest."

Helene bit her lower lip. "A little. How long will it feel like this?"

"For a few days. It won't be as painful tomorrow. I tried to make it as painless as possible, but unfortunately, the first few times are unpleasant for women."

"Thank you," Helene squeaked. "For being gentle."

His heart jumped inside his chest and he actually felt his cheeks grow hot. This girl was making him blush like an idiot schoolboy. "Don't thank me," he finally managed to say gruffly as he reached for her clothing. "We made an agreement. Now, let's get you dressed. It's time to take you home."

Chapter 6

*Z*achary could hear Helene's breasts bouncing against each other as his fingers gripped her fleshy hips. Her ass was nice, round, and slightly pink which made a pretty picture as he pounded into her from behind.

Helene was on all fours on his large bed while Zachary entered her slowly. This was only their second meeting and she was still getting used to his length, though she was a much better student than he had thought she was going to be.

He thought she was going to be scared once he had taken her virginity, but the redhead had turned up once again with the maid's uniform and a determined look on her face. Maybe she was one of the rare upper-class ladies who did enjoy making love to men and didn't find it a bothersome endeavor.

It was a pleasant surprise.

Zachary had placed a mirror in front of them, much to Helene's embarrassment. He wanted to study Helene's facial features and stop when it became too much for her. Helene was too stubborn to actually tell him anything.

But he didn't notice any pain on the redhead's face. In fact, he didn't notice anything but pleasure, which made his dick grow hard again even though he was already inside her. Helene's face was bright red, her mouth was slightly parted as she panted, her red curls stuck to her forehead.

For someone who had never had sex before, the younger Miss Hollis sure learned quickly. Her blue eyes shone with lust every time she made her way up the stairs in her ridiculous maid's uniform.

So far, they only met once a week, but Zachary was tempted to make it every day. It seemed he couldn't get enough of her gorgeous little body. She was like an enchantress with him, tempting him with every move she made. He was almost sorry she was going to marry someone else.

His hand dipped between her legs where he found her weepy clit. She was soaked through, and her juices were dripping onto the French sheets. Zachary started rubbing her engorged clit with each of his thrusts, focusing on pressing the pad of his thumb directly at the center of her nerve endings.

Helene let out a moan of delight as she tumbled onto the front of the bed, giving Zachary a generous glimpse of her ass. Their pants were the only thing heard in the room before Helene asked, "Am I getting better?"

For some reason, the question annoyed Zachary. It was a reminder he was preparing a mare for another stallion. He slapped her bottom harder than necessary, leaving behind a pink handprint. Helene whimpered. "Go to sleep and stop asking unnecessary questions. I will wake you up when it's time to leave."

Helene nodded, looking at him with hurt eyes because she had been spanked. Zachary sighed as he motioned her to come forward. It was like dealing with a spoiled pet. "Come here."

A smile crossed her lips as she did as she was told, snuggling against his naked chest. He shouldn't be doing this. He knew how clingy women could get, but he couldn't deny how much he liked Helene's warm body against his.

Zachary had to admit this wouldn't be the worst way to wake up every morning. His father had been pestering him about finding a wife. Maybe it was finally time to listen to the old man.

"Let's go for a walk."

Helene furrowed her brow. "Now?" She looked down at her naked body which was barely covered with the sheet. Her nipples were hard little pebbles as they rubbed against his slightly hairy chest.

He smiled. "No, not now, silly I don't want anyone to see you like this." The idea of another man seeing her naked, even the future husband he was going to help her catch, made him see red. "I'll stop by your house at eleven o'clock, before lunch. Do you think your mother would mind?"

Helene raised an eyebrow. "Mother? On the contrary, she will be thrilled."

The next day, Zachary arrived to pick up Helene ten minutes before the allotted time. The Hollises' butler greeted him, seeming surprised when he announced he was here to see Helene. He couldn't help but feel annoyed at his attitude. Helene was just as beautiful as her sisters and should be given the same courtesy. If he had been the Eastons' butler, he would have fired him for the disrespect.

"Mr. Easton."

Both Hollis women turned to stare at him when he was

announced. Like a mischievous toddler, Helene was pretending to read. She was dressed in a narrow, dark blue gown, with a cinched waist which matched the shade of her eyes. He had to admit he loved seeing her in blue.

Mrs. Hollis was needlepointing across from her daughter, looking surprised to see him. Zachary had only had a few conversations with the Hollis sisters' mother. He found her to be an odious woman who cared too much about the family's reputation and who liked to remind people she was the third cousin of an English viscount.

Zachary kissed the back of the hands of both Mrs. Hollis and Miss Hollis. When her mother's back was turned, Helene winked at him.

He smiled. It was like they were having their own private joke.

"Mr. Easton, how lovely to see you. Do come in. Please wait a minute while I ring for some refreshments." Mrs. Hollis rang a tiny bell and a young maid came rushing in with tea and cookies. No doubt Mrs. Hollis had already threatened to fire the poor girl if she was less than perfect.

After they had settled in with their tea and cookies and Zachary had complimented Mrs. Hollis on her lovely home, he decided to announce what he was here for. "Mrs. Hollis, thank you for your lovely hospitality. The reason I came to visit is because I was wondering if you will permit me to go on a walk with Miss Hollis?"

Mrs. Hollis blinked. "A walk?"

"Yes, there is a park close by. I haven't seen Miss Hollis much since I returned from Harvard and the weather is lovely. I thought she would fancy a walk with me. If you approve, of course."

Helene touched her mother's hand. "Please, Mother. The weather is so lovely."

"All right, dear, do not make a fuss." Then she turned

stern as she looked at her guest. "Thank you for the lovely invitation, Mr. Easton, I'm sure my daughter will appreciate it. I cannot chaperone because my legs are not what they used to be, but I will send my maid, Pearl, in my place. I expect you to bring my daughter home by lunchtime."

That was in forty-five minutes.

Zachary nodded as he stood up and offered a hand to Helene. "Understood, Mrs. Hollis. Do not worry, your daughter will be safe and sound with me."

After paying the maid, Pearl, to sit on a bench in the nearby park instead of following along with them, Zachary and Helene started on their walk. Helene played with her parasol, twirling it around. "What did you want to talk about that we couldn't discuss in your bedroom?"

He cleared his throat. "Well, as we agreed, I will be picking the suitor that you will marry. However, you still have not told me what kind of man you would like as your future husband. What are some of the qualities you are looking for?"

Helene bit her lip; it was obvious she had never really thought about it. She just wanted to be married. Figures. Women never think beyond an elaborate ceremony, which wasn't surprising. Zachary knew couples who barely talked for more than three sentences after they had been wed.

"Well, I suppose I would like him to be decent-looking, have all his teeth." Zachary smiled. "He needs to come from a decent and old family, to serve Mother's preference. I would like him to be kind and funny. I don't want to be married to a dull man. Oh, and I don't want him to be with other women after we've wed."

He frowned. "The last one might be difficult." Many men had extramarital affairs after marriage. Poor or rich.

"My sisters' husbands are loyal."

"Corinne and Audrina's husbands are possessive to the point of being ridiculous. There are not many men like that."

"Well, I want one," she replied stubbornly, crossing her arms over her ample chest.

He sighed. "I'll see what I can do."

"I'm sure there are other men who are capable of showing the same devotion Nicholas Barrett and Dominic Darlington have for my sisters." Helene narrowed her eyes at him. "It is your job to find a loyal husband for me, is it not?"

"I told you I would help you snag a husband, I never promised loyalty." He gritted his teeth. "You are asking me to do the impossible, I hope you know that."

After he dropped a grouchy Helene back home, Zachary found himself going to the gentlemen's club he often frequented. On the way over, he tried thinking of loyal married men or currently unwed men who he was sure would never cheat on his wife. He couldn't think of any.

For a moment, Zachary thought about lying to Helene and selling her the idea of the perfect, loyal man until she wed. But the idea of seeing her pretty, heartbroken face made him melt into a puddle of guilt.

Despite her stubbornness, Helene was a sweet girl and she didn't deserve a disloyal fool. But what if that's all there was to offer? He wasn't too hopeful that his sister Kathleen would be able to find a loyal man, either, even though he was pretty sure he would kill any man who would harm his sister.

The gentlemen's club he frequented was nearly empty, as most men didn't come until after dinner, to get away from their wives. He ordered a whisky from one of the passing waiters before he settled in a nearby, comfortable leather chair. It wouldn't be long before men flocked to him.

He was right.

Two men, Carl Ashton, who was the fool who had stolen Helene from the dance floor, and Robert Wells, who had attended boarding school with him, greeted him. Carl looked visibly drunk as if he hadn't learned how to control his liquor yet. The top button of Robert's trousers was undone. No doubt these two had come from a brothel or their mistresses' fancy apartments which they paid for.

Zachary gave them a brittle smile. He didn't consider himself a prude, but lately, he had found himself less patient with men. Perhaps it was because he had been forced to play matchmaker. Or maybe it was because he was starting to feel that he would never find a worthwhile match for Helene.

Each man seemed worse than the last.

Robert grinned at him. "May we join you?"

Zachary nodded, pointing his whisky glass to the two empty leather chairs.

Robert patted Carl on the shoulder when he didn't move. Carl let out a burp before he followed suit.

"Did you two gentleman have a nice evening? Or are you barely starting it?" Zachary took a sip of his drink. He was going to need a stronger drink if he was going to have to deal with these two fools all evening.

"Barely starting." Carl let out another burp before he settled into the seat, obviously sleepy. "We've been at The French all evening, haven't we, Wells?"

Robert nodded eagerly, a dreamy look on his face. The French was a well-known whorehouse that wasn't as unheard of like these two men wanted it to be; even Helene knew about it. The whorehouse boasted about their French whores.

Zachary had outgrown the place by the time he was nineteen. He preferred American girls, especially if they were redheads.

"I don't need to hear about it," Zachary interrupted when Robert opened his mouth to speak.

Robert shifted in his seat. "Are you bedding anyone good, Zachary? You've been awfully quiet about the subject. Or have you gotten yourself a mistress in your old age?"

"No. I haven't been with any women lately. Bedding a strange woman every night has become tiresome." *Especially since I would much prefer having Helene in my bed every night.*

Carl looked at him curiously, reminding Zachary how young he was. "Don't tell me you are behaving because you are looking for a wife?"

Many men often behaved like good Samaritans when shopping for a bride, only to return to bedding strangers after their honeymoon.

"Perhaps I am," Zachary lied.

He had no intention of marrying soon. His father would probably weep for joy and any mother with an unmarried daughter would probably be throwing themselves at him for the chance of their daughters becoming Mrs. Easton.

Robert nodded as if he understood. "Understandable. You need an heir since you don't have a brother, in case—" Robert chuckled nervously when Zachary glared at him. "Excellent decision, Easton. Every man should settle down with a wife and a baby at some point. You'll have your pick of the litter. Anyone you have in mind?"

Zachary wanted to bite his tongue, or at the very least, turn away and go in the opposite direction without muttering Helene's name. But he had promised Helene he would do this; they had a deal that he would get her a husband and Lord knew Zachary wasn't ready for marriage.

He held the whisky glass so stiffly, he was surprised he didn't break it. "Helene Hollis."

Carl and Robert blinked at him in confusion. They hadn't expected that. They probably thought he was going to say one of the Smith girls.

"Helene Hollis?" Robert cocked his head to the side. "Who is that?"

"The redhead," Carl pointed out helpfully. "The youngest Hollis sister."

"Ah, yes, the single Hollis daughter." Robert looked on in contemplation as if he couldn't remember Helene even if they had been part of the same social circle for years. "Is she part Irish will all that vibrant red hair?"

"I don't know," Zachary replied moodily. He wanted to punch the disgruntled look off Robert's face. His look told Zachary he didn't approve of his choice. But he didn't know Helene as well as Zachary did. Helene was much better than any of the Smith girls or any New York girl for that matter. She was clever, funny, and when she wasn't being so damn pushy and stubborn, she could be down-right adorable. Robert should thank his lucky stars if Helene ever looked in his direction.

But, of course, he couldn't say that, otherwise, people would grow suspicious. If anyone ever found out Zachary and Helene had been intimate before marriage, then both of their reputations would be ruined. He might leave unscathed as he was a man, but it would affect his little sister's marriage prospects.

"She's not bad looking," Carl pointed out unhelpfully. "She has nice blue eyes."

"But she's not as pretty as Corinne and Audrina Hollis."

"Corinne and Audrina Hollis are pretty, but Helene is beautiful." Zachary wanted to slap himself as soon as he said those words. He sounded like a lovesick fool. No self-respecting man would talk about a woman like that, even if he was thinking about courting her. "She will be a good wife to anyone who weds her."

"She is a good dancer," Carl grumbled after a while. "At least she doesn't step on my feet and she can manage a decent conversation which doesn't revolve around the weather."

Carl studied Zachary's face as if he was searching for something. It irritated him. "Are you courting Miss Hollis? Is she the lady you want to wed?"

Zachary didn't like the look on Carl's face. He looked like the cat who swallowed the canary. But perhaps he was exaggerating; he was weirdly protective of Helene after all. He shook his head. "Helene has not looked twice in my direction. She is destined for someone else."

Chapter 7

"Today, I am going to teach you how to pleasure a man with your mouth," Zachary instructed the next time he and Helene met, which was a few weeks later. They had both grown more comfortable with each other's presence, even if his servants thought he was rather odd because he locked himself in his bedroom for a few hours every week. With strict instructions not to come up under any circumstances, of course, even though he sometimes felt Helene's screams could be heard down the street.

A fact which made him weirdly proud.

Helene, who was still dressed in her horrid maid's uniform, raised her hand like a dutiful student. "Yes?"

"My friend, Rose, spoke of this. That is when a woman kisses the head of a man's cock, right?"

The expression on her face was so serious and adorable that he couldn't help but laugh. Perhaps these society girls weren't as quiet and sweet as they let on. Zachary couldn't believe some of the insane notions Helene had about sex.

Some of them were true, while others seemed to come out of an insane storybook.

"Sometimes. Though there is usually more than kissing involved."

"I see. Does a woman bite it?" There was a mischievous look in Helene's eyes so Zachary couldn't tell if she was truly clueless or not, but really, with a sister like Corinne, how innocent could she be?

Helene had surprised Zachary these past few weeks with the knowledge she had gained and the pleasure both of them received. She was hardly the proper little miss she had been a few weeks ago, and truth be told, Zachary preferred it. He would have been much more annoyed if she had been blushing and stuttering the entire time.

"Not unless you want blood in your mouth and a spanked rump."

Helene pouted. "Then how do you perform oral pleasure on a man?"

Zachary stretched in his seat, already getting hard. Helene had the special ability to make his body long for her with just a simple question. He was lucky he didn't soil his trousers with his seed beforehand. He suddenly longed to finish inside her; nothing would give him more pleasure than to fill her sweet quim with his milk.

Unfortunately, Zachary had no interest in being a father, and a baby was too much of a risk that he couldn't take. He had to be satisfied with finishing in his hand or on his expensive sheets for now.

"Zachary, are you listening?" she asked, annoyed.

"Get on your knees in front of me," he ordered hoarsely.

Helene did as she was told without complaining, placing herself in front on him. Damn it, his trousers felt uncomfortably tight and he still hadn't undressed. With her maid's outfit and her big doe eyes, Helene Hollis was starting to look like an irresistible temptation.

"I'm going to teach you how to please a man, no biting," he warned her and she nodded.

He started undressing himself so that only his cock was visible. If he undressed himself completely, he would end up bending her over the table and burying himself inside her before he could teach her how to pleasure him with her mouth.

Zachary felt dirty, as if he were committing a crime. Helene was too pretty and innocent for him. He should dress himself, take her to her parents, and confess about the affair they had been having for weeks, disguised as a matchmaking scheme.

But if he refused her, then Helene would be pigheaded enough to go find another man to train her. A man who would not be as discreet as Zachary. With Helene's luck, she would find herself married to the creep. The idea filled him with jealousy and dread at another man having her. It was ridiculous, of course, since she would marry a man of Zachary's choosing.

Zachary wondered how long he could prevent Helene from getting married without her getting suspicious.

"Zachary," she prompted, clearly annoyed.

He loved the way she said his name even when she sounded annoyed. He would work on getting her to scream his name when they were in bed together. The thought made him almost wild with need.

"Be patient, brat," he scolded her. She flushed bright pink which made her all the more adorable.

Helene was staring at his cock as if waiting for it to come alive. His manhood twitched and she nearly jumped a foot. He laughed. "It's been inside of you before, Hel. Don't you remember?"

"I've never seen it up close before," she argued with him.

He laughed softly as he placed a hand on top of her head. "Just relax, sweetheart, you will be all right. I'll guide you through everything. Now, stay still." Helene did as she was told. "Now, part those pretty lips. I'm going to insert my cock inside your mouth. If you feel uncomfortable at all during the process, let me know, and I'll stop. Understood?"

She nodded, her lips parting, allowing him to thrust himself in.

Zachary entered his cock slowly in, between her gorgeous pink lips. Her eyes widened at the fullness she was feeling. He placed a hand on top of her head, rummaging it through her red curls. "Be a good girl and relax for me," he ordered.

When he felt her relax, he pushed the last remaining inches inside her. Helene let out a small choking sound which only caused his cock to bounce inside her mouth. "Now remember, no biting. Just suck. Run your tongue down the sides of my cock and on the tip. Take your time, Hel."

Helene did as she was told, like the good little student that she was. She ran her tongue up and down the base of his cock, covering every inch with her daring little tongue, Then she sucked in her cheeks and started sucking, focusing specifically on his tip, as if she were a cat determined to get every ounce of milk from its bowl.

Zachary stiffened, then he closed his eyes, gripping her red hair. This felt wonderful. She was a complete natural.

"Good girl, Hel. I need you to stop and pull out now. I don't want to finish inside your mouth. It's not proper." As if any part of their little agreement was proper.

Helene seemed to think the same thing because she

threw him a confused face before she ignored him and continued sucking until he exploded in her mouth. Hot cum spilled down her lips and chin while a proud little expression started forming on Helene's face.

Zachary pulled out of her mouth; it felt good finishing inside one part of her even when where he really wanted to finish was in her tight quim.

Helene looked pleased by the sensation. She was licking her lower lip in a way that made him hard all over again. She looked up at him unexpectedly, like an adorable deer waiting for a second command.

But he couldn't make love to her, not tonight. He was desperate enough to be inside her, and with his luck would end up in a pregnancy because he didn't pull away in time.

"You need to head home," he said rudely as he fixed his trousers.

Helene blinked, confused, but eventually nodded. "This was a very short lesson," she complained as she smoothed down her dress.

"Are you a glutton for punishment, Miss Hollis?"

"No, I just want to get every penny's worth of lessons," she replied sweetly.

"You're not paying me."

"Oh, I am. I see the way you look at me, Zachary, when you think I'm not looking."

He was surprised at her cheekiness. She had definitely gotten more bold with him as the weeks had gone by. It was surprisingly adorable.

"Nevertheless, it's time you leave. I have to see my father."

"Why?"

"He wants to plan a ball, and since Mother is dead and my sister has no clue what she's doing, I'm afraid I'm the only one who can assist him."

"Not the armful of servants he has at his disposal?"

"Father is very particular and, at times, not the brightest, I'm afraid."

Helene nodded as she rearranged the maid's cap on her head. "Who is the party for?"

"Kathleen. Father is worried she's too shy to stand out against the other girls. He's hoping a ball where she plays the part of hostess would be a more viable way for her to catch a husband."

Kathleen Easton was quite pretty, but she was also terribly shy and preferred to hide in the corner of ballrooms with Helene. She had barely made it during her own debut ball without fainting and she had been a nervous mess at the end if she recalled correctly.

"I'm sure Kathleen will be thrilled," Helene replied sarcastically and he responded by smacking her on the rump, which caused her to squeal. Helene rubbed her bottom while staring at him angrily. "Am I invited?"

He looked surprised. "Of course, why wouldn't you be?"

She shrugged. "I just thought you would want to focus on finding your sister a husband instead of me. It *is* her ball, after all."

Zachary frowned. He had forgotten he had promised Helene to take the lead in her ridiculous husband hunting endeavors. He just never thought he would have to do it at his own house. It would be like inviting random people to steal his food.

"I can handle finding husbands for the both of you," he answered curtly, feeling annoyed.

Truth be told, he was going to focus on Helene. He trusted his sister when it came to picking husbands. She had a good head on her shoulders and would not pick anyone who was not good for her. Helene, on the other hand, was flighty and, like most women, didn't suspect the bad in people. He would never be able to forgive himself if he picked a lousy husband for her.

Helene gave him a funny look and he wondered what she was thinking. Probably something rude or obnoxious. Noticing he wasn't in the mood to talk, she decided to take her leave. "I will see you at the ball."

The next few days were horrendous for Zachary; it just felt like one problem falling on his lap after another. His father kept changing the menu for the ball, the servants were irritable because they had to make such vast changes to the Eastons' ballroom in so little time, and Kathleen was in near tears at being expected to play hostess for the duration of the entire night.

He just couldn't wait for the stupid thing to be over and done with.

"We should have gone with the lamb instead," Mr. Easton muttered next to him. The three of them were standing by the doorway, ready to greet the guests.

"Chicken is fine, Father."

"Peasants feed their guests chicken. I won't have the guests think Kathleen comes from a low breed family who can't afford a decent menu for a ball."

"I doubt peasants have chicken, Father."

"Then what do they eat, since you apparently know so much?"

"Bread and cheese or butter, I suppose. Chicken, perhaps on Christmas."

"Will you two be quiet!" Kathleen huffed beside them. She was dressed in a pale orange gown with white lace, which made her look like a fluffy peach. Her cheeks were flushed and there was perspiration clinging to her face. Only half of the guests had arrived and she was already a puddle of nerves. If she managed to get through the entire party without fainting, it would be a miracle.

"Mr. and Mrs. Hollis and Miss Hollis."

Zachary looked up and saw Helene in a light blue dress which was almost silvery. Her red hair was done in tight ringlets in a half updo, complete with fresh flowers. After greeting her parents, Zachary pressed his lips to the back of her gloved hand. It felt weird greeting her like a polite stranger when she had been in his bed at least once a week.

Helene giggled like a schoolgirl, which caused her mother to glare at her.

After the greeting of the guests came the dinner, with several fancy courses and a wide selection of fruits, cheese, and pastries before the guests were taken to the Eastons' ballroom. The guests gasped when they saw the room decorated with fine vases, fresh flowers, and ornate chandeliers. A group of musicians started to play at once.

Zachary opened the ball by dancing with his sister. It felt weird dancing in the Eastons' ballroom; they hadn't hosted balls since his mother had died. His father had been too depressed. Poor Kathleen was so nervous, she stepped on her brother's feet three times and both of them were relieved when the dance finally ended.

Out of pity, the musicians started to play another song once Zachary and Kathleen exited the center of the ballroom. Kathleen went to refresh herself, since the top of her dress was covered in perspiration, while Zachary went in search of Helene. He wanted to fill her dance card.

Around him, young women flirted with him by batting their eyelashes or moving their fans seductively. Usually, Zachary would at least humor them. Who would be able to say no to a pretty face? But now, the only thing he could think of was how much he wanted to see Helene.

He had expected to see her with the rest of the wallflowers, huddled in the small sitting area at the end of the ballroom. He checked the refreshment table and then asked a random young lady to search the ladies' resting area, but she was nowhere to be found.

A giggle, he turned around when he heard that giggling. He recognized it almost immediately. Helene. Her laughs and smiles haunted him almost daily now, much to his misfortune.

Helene was near the refreshment table which had been stationed next to a horrible statue his parents had bought in Milan during their honeymoon. Helene was surrounded by a handful of suitors, with her at the center. Her silvery blue dress glittered under the lights from the nearby chandeliers and candles.

She looked like a star.

Zachary couldn't help but be taken back. When he'd seen her in other instances, he had always found her alone or with his sister. Now, she was the belle of the ball and not feeling the least bit shy.

It even looked like the men were fighting for her attention by bringing her glasses of whatever the Eastons were serving as drinks while others went to grasp the frail dance card which hung from her wrist. A dance card which already seemed full.

A tinge of annoyance went through Zachary's body. Why was she even entertaining this group of dull men? They were beneath her, she should know that. None of them would make good husbands.

Zachary forced himself into the center of the intimate circle until he was standing face to face with Helene. Out of the corner of his eye, he saw Mrs. Hollis stare back at her daughter. She didn't seem to know if she should be horrified or impressed by the situation.

"Zach!" she practically yelled. "I thought you went to bed!"

Her face was bright pink, which usually meant she'd had more than enough to drink, and she was also slurring her words.

"Stop giving her drinks!" Zachary ignored her as he snapped at Christopher Davenport who had just been about to offer her another drink. Christopher stumbled, nearly spilling the drink on himself like the idiot that he was.

Helene pouted.

"I think you've had enough to drink," he said coldly, turning back to the redhead.

She just shrugged.

It took every ounce of restraint in him not to place her over his knee and give her the whipping she deserved. She shouldn't be drunk around men.

He took a deep breath, begging the Lord for patience. He could see the men around him staring at him with curiosity, wondering why he was there, while others were looking at him as if he were competition. Zachary almost wanted to tell them that there was no competition when he had already won.

"I came to fill out your dance card. If you would do me the honor, Miss Hollis," he replied rudely.

Helene wiggled the dance card in the air. "My dance card is all filled out, I'm afraid, Mr. Easton."

Zachary gritted his teeth.

A man clapped him on the shoulder. "That's the downside of being a host, Easton. You never have any fun."

Zachary fought the urge to punch him until he lost all his teeth.

Carl bowed shyly in front of Helene. "Miss Hollis, I'm first on your list. I believe it's time for our dance."

Helene nodded as she offered her gloved hand. "Please lead the way, sir."

Zachary broke away from the crowd of men to watch Helene and Carl dance. His sister joined him a second later, wearing a fresh pair of gloves. "They look lovely together," she commented.

Zachary grimaced as he took in the way Carl gripped her waist and said something stupid to make her smile. Seeing her dance with man after man for hours, would be pure torture. "I'm going to bed. I'm not feeling well."

———

"What color are you getting for your new dress?" Kathleen asked as they walked arm in arm to the modiste they simply referred to as Miss Belle. It was a lovely day outside and both young women decided to walk while both of their maids trailed behind them.

It was a few days after the Eastons' ball, and Helene had sent a note to her friend asking her if she wanted to go shopping for new evening gowns. Kathleen had readily accepted, saying she needed some fresh air after what she felt was her disastrous ball.

Helene didn't share the same sentiment. She and her mother had been positively ecstatic following the Eastons' ball. They had been receiving invitations for new balls, soirées, and luncheons almost daily. It was the first time she had been so popular. Mrs. Hollis had actually been the one to suggest the trip to the modiste in the first place.

Her cheeks flushed with pleasure as she thought about how the men had gathered around her like a heavenly circle. She hadn't needed Zachary's help at the ball, after all. All the men had flocked over to her like happy bees among a fresh rose.

Helene didn't see Zachary for the rest of the ball, but she hadn't minded. She had been too busy dancing with different gentlemen, and balls weren't exactly Zachary's favorite activity.

"I'm thinking red," Helene finally answered. Her mother would have a coronary if she showed up with a red dress which matched her red locks.

Kathleen looked perplexed. "Red, like Corinne's color?"

Helene snorted. "The color red doesn't belong to my sister. A lot of other girls wear red evening gowns."

"I know, but your sister was known for her red dresses."

That part was true, while Helene and Audrina had always opted for soft blues or greens, Corinne had always worn red. It was her signature color. When they had lived in the same house, her closet had been stuffed full with dresses in different shades of red.

"I just want to try it," Helene said, growing annoyed. "I'm so sick of blue."

"But you love blue."

"I love other colors as well."

Kathleen didn't say anything more, she just followed Helene inside the shop. Miss Belle was fluttering around like a butterfly, holding two sewing needles between her lips while carrying two bolts of cloth. She nodded her greeting, letting them know she would be with them shortly.

While they waited, Helene looked around the thick bolts of cloth and the half-finished dresses. She wasn't quite sure what she wanted, but she knew she wanted it to be unforgettable. Her ball gowns so far had been prim and proper, which, according to her mother, was the proper way to catch a husband, but she seemed to get more attention when she was showing a bit of cleavage.

She stopped in front of a bolt of red cloth which reminded her of bright cherries. A smile crossed her lips. This was the color she wanted. If her mother had a fit because the color clashed with her hair, then she would just remind her how popular Corinne had been with the color.

"Thank you for waiting, how may I help you, Miss Hollis, Miss Easton?" Miss Belle sounded exhausted as she rested her back against the bolts of clothes. Miss Belle and her mother were the same age, but she had never seen her mother as frazzled as Miss Belle. Then again, Mrs. Hollis had never had to work, and neither had any of the Hollis sisters, with the exception of Audrina, who had worked for a bit while running away from her fiancé.

"I just need a new nightgown and some underthings," Kathleen replied as she played with her curls. "And a new ballgown."

Miss Belle nodded. "I have some lovely new things I can show you, Miss Easton. I already have your measurements on file, so I can have your things ready by the end of the week except for the dress. What can I do for you, Miss Hollis?"

"I would like an evening gown with this cloth." Helene pointed to the cherry red cloth.

Miss Belle nodded. "Red, your sister's color."

"It's not my sister's color, anyone can wear red." Helene shut her mouth. She sounded childish. "Do you have any designs you could show me? I will need the dress in two weeks." One of her mother's charities was hosting a large ball to help fund the construction of a new museum. It would be crawling with gentlemen, the perfect place to find a husband.

Miss Belle nodded as she flipped through a larger sketchbook of designs. She finally choose one which she thought would be perfect. The dress would have a tight bodice, show off more of her milky white shoulders than appropriate, and have a long row of buttons which would draw attention to her long neck and slim shoulders.

Miss Belle promised to be done in two weeks, thankfully ignoring Helene's snippy attitude from earlier. Afterwards, Kathleen begged her to accompany her to a shoe store in order to get her father a nice pair for his birthday in a few months.

While Kathleen made her order to the man behind the counter, Helene entertained herself with the rows of men's shoes. The styles were different, but the colors were the same. How did men not get bored wearing the same dreary colors?

Helene was pretending to be interested in a pair of men's shoes when she felt someone bumping into her. "Oh, pardon me." She stopped short when she recognized the glossy dark hair and the broad back. "Zachary!"

Zachary gave her a curt nod, not at all perplexed that she was standing in the men's section of the shoe store. "Miss Hollis."

"What are you doing here?"

He pointed curtly to where his valet was picking up his purchases. "Same as you. I assume you came to accompany my sister?"

She nodded. It seemed like Zachary was struggling to hold a decent conversation with her, almost like he couldn't wait to get rid of her. Perhaps he didn't want to risk anyone being suspicious, but the store was nearly empty with the exception of Kathleen, who was driving the salesman insane because she kept changing her mind every five seconds.

They hadn't set up another date for when they were going to meet, but Helene hoped it would be soon. She missed being close to Zachary and smelling his sweet-smelling soap. She also wouldn't say no to having him between her legs again.

"I missed you at the ball. Kathleen said you were feeling ill. I hope you are feeling much better."

"Yes." Zachary looked distracted as he looked around the shop, refusing to look at Helene. "Though I don't believe you missed me too much, Miss Hollis, since your dance card was full."

She blinked. "That was the point, was it not? How can I find a husband if I don't dance with them?"

Zachary curled his lip, and before he could respond, Kathleen gripped his hand. "Oh, Zach, I'm so glad you're here. Please look at these, do you think Father will like them?"

"They are fine, Kat." Zachary kissed her forehead, ignoring Helene completely as if she were nothing more than a cockroach. It took everything in Helene not to stomp her feet like a little girl. "Enjoy your shopping trip, girls."

Before Helene could utter another word, he was gone, with his valet trailing after him. Helene huffed. "Why was he in such a horrid mood?"

Kathleen shrugged. "He's been a little tense lately. My father wants him to take over the business by next year, but Zach has always had a wandering foot. If it were up to him, he would be somewhere in Asia by now. Don't mind him, Helene. Men often have more foul tempers than women. Speaking of men, have you decided if you met any man you want to seriously court at my ball?"

Helene shrugged. She had been flattered at first by all the attention she had gotten, but none of the men had caught her attention. Not in the way Zachary had. In fact, she didn't feel fully comfortable in any of their presence. When she was with Zachary, they would often joke or tease each other, but with the men she danced with, she felt stiff and formal.

She shook her head. Helene shouldn't even be thinking about Zachary; there wasn't a less marriageable man in all of New York.

"I wish you would marry Zachary," Kathleen blurted out as she squeezed Helene with her gloved hand as they headed to the counter. "Then we would be sisters-in-law, wouldn't that be fun?" She then sighed. "But Zachary won't marry anytime soon. He's a stubborn mule."

Helene shrugged as she looked at the retreating door which Zachary had just left through. "That, he is."

Chapter 8

"**F**or you, Miss Hollis."

The Hollis butler held up a silver tray for her which contained a single, creamy envelope. She recognized the penmanship almost immediately. It was from Corinne. A letter all the way from England. She had been feeling a tad bitter that neither of her married sisters had bothered to write in weeks, but as soon as she had the letter in her hands, her anger had diminished.

She was alone in the sitting room with a half empty plate of cookies in front of her. All the lovemaking she and Zachary had been doing was making her hungry, not that she could tell anyone that, even though she was dying to. Helene couldn't believe she and Zachary had managed to hide their passionate affair for weeks now. She hadn't thought they would have gotten away with it, but she had been happily proven wrong.

Helene was suddenly thankful her mother was not in the sitting room. Mrs. Hollis was lying down in bed complaining of a headache while Mr. Hollis was meeting with his lawyer.

"Thank you, that will be all."

The butler nodded. "Very well, miss. Please let me know if you have a letter you would like to send to Mrs. Barrett or Mrs. Darlington through the evening post. I'll send Alfred to deliver it."

"Thank you."

Once Helene was alone again, she grabbed her sharp letter opener and nearly ripped apart the delicate English paper. In Corinne's delicate handwriting, she wrote:

Dearest Helene,

I must inform you about how happy I am to hear from Mother about your success in the marriage mart. I must admit you did surprise me. I never did believe you would be popular with the opposite sex, but you have proven me wrong.

Well done, little sister, there are few people who surprise me. Be happy you can be among the small list. Mother tells me that every ball you attend has you with suitors vying for your attention like they once were for me and Audrina. Your dance card is always full and there are rumors you will be the first in your set to wed.

Be proud of this, Helene, for there are few girls who are able to achieve such an honor. Listen to my warning, do not marry the first fool who comes along. A parrot can quite easily mimic the same words a fool man can.

Flirt, enjoy yourself, for you have never received such attention. But when choosing a husband, remember this, look for wealth, look for intelligence. Nothing is duller than a man who can't make proper conversation, and look for kindness. I must admit the last one I never thought of as important, but my marriage to Nicholas has made me soft.

As I wrote to Mother, I am heavily pregnant. I do hope this one is a boy, for Nicholas needs an heir, but he says he is happy with another girl and I believe him, for our daughter is the apple of his eye.

Clarissa is now walking and grows more beautiful every day. Nicholas is afraid I will make her as vain as I am. She is a sweet little thing; she reminds me of you, with her head in the clouds. I do hope Clarissa meets her Aunt Helene soon.

Nicholas and I wish to invite you to spend Christmas in England. That is if you're not married by then. Please write to Audrina, the dolt is sick with worry, thinking Mother and Father will marry you off like they did her. Our sister is glowing; impending motherhood suits her even if I can't stand her husband. He's even more insufferable than Nicholas ever was.

Sending you all my love,
Corinne Hollis Barrett

Helene smiled to herself as she read the letter two more times. It was nice hearing that Corinne missed her. As the youngest, she was often left out of Audrina and Corinne's more grown-up conversations. It was nice that they missed her. She longed to see her sisters and niece, but, oh why did they have to live so far away?

The redhead read the letter a third time to confirm Corinne's praise. She didn't remember the last time she had been praised by her eldest sister. She should probably frame the letter. This was probably the only time she would impress her.

Helene removed the fallen cookie crumbles from her dress before she went towards her writing desk. If she hurried and wrote her response back, Alfred might be able to send it by evening post. She couldn't wait to spend Christmas with her sisters. She didn't think her parents would say no since she had been doing so well in getting new suitors instead of hiding like a wallflower. Besides, she doubted she would be married by December.

Corinne was right about one thing; she had to choose

her suitors carefully, even though she had agreed Zachary would make the final choice. Helene made a mental note to ask Zachary if he had anyone in mind for a potential husband the next time they met.

Helene was halfway through her letter when the butler entered the room again. "Oh, I am not quite done with my letter."

"Not to worry Miss Hollis. I came to inform you a package arrived for you."

"A package?"

"Well, a gift might be the better word."

"What kind of gift?"

The butler pursed his lips, obviously uncomfortable. "May I bring it in, Miss Hollis, so you may see it for yourself?"

Helene nodded eagerly. This was the first time she had received a present from a non-family member.

The Hollis butler came back, seemingly annoyed that he had to deal with Helene at all when he already had to deal with her troublesome mother. In his arms, he was holding a large blue vase with pink and blue flowers. She thought they were the most beautiful thing she had ever seen.

Trailing behind him, was Kathleen who looked equally glad at the prospect of her best friend being sent flowers. "Miss Kathleen Easton," he announced sourly as he placed the bouquet on the table next to Helene. "For you, miss." He gave a quick bow, indicating he had no interest in being called again.

"Who are they from?" Kathleen inquired as she sat across from her after kissing her cheek. "Is there a card?"

"I don't know. Who would send me flowers?" She hoped it was Zachary; who else would send her flowers? She didn't know how Kathleen would react if it was

Zachary. She loved her brother and she loved Helene, but Helene didn't know if Kathleen would approve of them being together, even though she had mentioned it in passing.

With trembling fingers, she picked up the creamy card. If it was from Zachary, she hoped her best friend would approve. She wouldn't be able to bear it if her best friend Kathleen didn't think she was good enough for her brother.

When Helene finally got the card open, she didn't know if she should be relieved or disappointed by who it was from.

Katheen leaned forward, her bosom nearly pouring from her cinched dress. "What does it say? Who is it from?"

"It's from Carl Ashton. The card says 'These flowers are as lovely as you, dear Miss Hollis. Sincerely, Carl Ashton.'"

Kathleen tried to hide her disappointment by giving her a small smile. "Well, he is certainly acceptable. His older brother married the elder Vanderbilt cousin, I believe."

"Third cousin," Helene corrected as she let the card fall, unable to hide her disappointment. The Ashtons were an old family, like theirs. Why, their grandfather had created their shipping empire in less than a year, which still rendered people speechless to this day. Her parents and sisters would have approved of the match, so why wasn't she happy? She could do far worse than being Mrs. Ashton. The Ashtons had several homes in England, so she could visit Corinne and Audrina.

"You don't seem happy," Kathleen announced gently. "You could do far worse than Carl Ashton. Haven't you two talked before?"

"We've danced," Helene corrected, obviously unhappy. "Twice. He kept looking at his feet the entire time. He just isn't the man I thought I would marry."

Kathleen laughed. "You are just like my brother."

"How so?"

"Well, Zachary says he will not marry anyone he is not in love with. Which I believe is rather a delusional way of thinking. Love for people like us rarely happens in the courting stage. We have to wait until after marriage for love to blossom."

"You sound like an old woman; it's terribly unromantic."

"Perhaps, but it keeps your heart from being broken." Kathleen gave her a sad smile. "You know I'm right, Helene. Girls like us, especially, cannot afford to be too picky."

Kathleen meant plain, uninteresting wallflowers like the both of them. Kathleen was pretty enough, but she was hopelessly shy to the point she could hardly have a conversation without stuttering. Helene was a wonderful dancer, but her bluntness and bright red hair often kept people away for girls who were more traditionally pretty.

Helene felt as if her friend had slapped her, even if she was only being honest. "I know."

"He's a nice man," Kathleen tried to desperately soften the blow. She knew how sensitive Helene was. "He could make you very happy if you just let him. Besides, if gentlemen find out he is sending you flowers, you might get more suitors. Regina Mills says men always want what other men want more."

Helene was brightened at the thought. Yes, this was quite possibly the first of many suitors. If men found out that Carl was sending her flowers, then perhaps others would and she could have the pick of any man she wanted.

She looked at the flowers again, hope rising in her chest. This was just the beginning.

Kathleen stayed for tea, and after she left, Helene snuck outside of her home instead of going upstairs to change for dinner. She wouldn't be gone long and her parents were going out to dinner again. She had told her maid that she wasn't feeling well and didn't want to be disturbed, not even for food.

It felt weird being outside without a maid or in a stage-coach when she was in her normal clothes. Her mother didn't approve of her walking down the streets of New York even in broad daylight hours. She would have a coronary if she saw Helene now, but really, Zachary's house wasn't far away.

Out of precaution, she had worn her thick blue coat even though she was sweating in it because it had a large hood which could cover her head. Her excitement grew, the more steps she took. Her disappointment about Carl faded as she approached Zachary's home. Yes, Carl wasn't her dream match, but he wasn't a complete toad, either. Kathleen was right, admirers would come before she knew it.

She hoped Zachary would be excited for her.

Helene decided against going through the servants' entrance as she would be much more noticeable than in the maid's outfit she regularly wore. She knew Zachary's servants' schedules by now and knew Zachary allowed them to have an early dinner before they served him a tray in his bedroom. He didn't like eating alone at the dining room table which is why he often ate dinner at the club.

Once she was inside, Helene went quietly up the stairs, trying her best not to make a peep. This was kind of fun, she thought as she bit back a giggle as she made her way up to Zachary's room. The door was closed and she timidly knocked on the door.

"Zachary?"

When he didn't answer, Helene opened the door. The room was dark and not a single candle was lit. She found Zachary sleeping on his bed, looking relatively peaceful.

Helene couldn't help but smile. This was the first time she had seen him asleep and he looked almost adorable. He always seemed uptight when he was around Helene, like the stern professors she had read about in novels.

Feeling in a teasing mode, Helene pressed her lips to his forehead.

Zachary opened his eyes immediately, wide with obvious shock. It took him a moment to register her presence. "Helene?"

She nodded. "Oh, Zachary, the most wonderful thing just happened, I just had to come here and tell you."

Zachary rose almost immediately, anger clearly on his face. He gripped both of her upper arms in a way that he had never done before, except perhaps when they were making love. "What the hell are you doing here?" He looked at her fine clothes. "Especially dressed like that. Where is your maid's outfit?"

Her lower lip trembled. She had never seen Zachary so angry; he was usually more carefree than most men. "I forgot it. I wasn't planning on staying here long. I just had something to tell you. It wasn't going to take long, so I didn't think it would be a big issue—"

"Did anyone see you?" he hissed. "In the streets, or when you were coming up the stairs?"

"No, of course not."

"Are you absolutely positive? Could you swear on it?"

Helene closed her mouth tightly. She could not guarantee anything. "No, but I was wearing my hood and I was very careful."

This didn't seem to please Zachary who looked like he wanted to strangle her. "Can you swear that no one has even seen a slip of your skirt?"

Helene flushed but slowly shook her head. She no longer felt excited about Carl's flowers. "No."

"Do you remember what I told you would happen if you ever stormed into my house without your disguise?" he asked quietly. His voice was soft, but a chill had definitely gone down her spine.

"You said I would be spanked," she announced quietly.

Zachary nodded as he pushed an antique French chair in front of her.

Her eyes watered. "Please don't spank me. I'll be good. I promise I will never come in my regular clothes again."

"Helene, we made an agreement," he said sternly. "Now, you can take your spanking like a good girl, or we can stop seeing each other. No more training. No more pleasantries. Nothing but a single hello when Kathleen drags us into the same room. Understood?"

She nodded slowly. Helene didn't want to get spanked, but she also didn't want to go back to the ways things were. Helene and Zachary would never go back to the ways things were before. Even when both of them were married, they would still remember the time they had spent together.

"I'll take the spanking," she whispered quietly.

He nodded, obviously approving of her choice. "Bend over."

Helene slowly made her way towards the chair, bending over the hard surface, the chair digging into her belly. She felt more nervous now than when Zachary took her virginity.

She stiffened when she felt Zachary pull up her skirts and petticoats. Thankfully, she was in her simple day dress and wasn't wearing too many underthings. Her drawers pooled at her legs. Air stung her bare rump, reminding her that it would not remain like that for long.

Helene flinched when she heard Zachary take off his belt and wrap it in half to get ready to whip her. "Oh, please, Zach, don't use your belt. It will hurt a lot."

"A spanking is supposed to hurt, Hel. I used my hand last time, now you're getting the belt for the same offense."

Helene's lower lip trembled, but she didn't argue. She stiffened a bit when she felt his fine, leather belt being pressed in the center of both cheeks. When he removed it, Helene shut her eyes tightly.

The belt landed with a loud crack, hitting the center of her rear end. Helene gasped at the sudden sting. This was worse than being spanked with his hand. The belt fell again, first on the back of her thighs, then on the upper part of her bottom, near her hips.

Helene cried out. Her bottom felt like it was on fire, as if it had been left in the sun for too long. She gripped the end of the chair; otherwise, she was going to start flailing her arms and begging pathetically.

The belting continued, the leather biting into her sensitive cheeks rapidly. Her ass bounced with each whip of the implement until she was sure it was colored a bright red color. It was growing hotter underneath the belt's administration and she wouldn't be surprised if it was swollen.

Helene sobbed over the chair as Zachary roasted her bottom. There wasn't any point in begging for mercy—if Zachary thought she should be punished, then she would be. She had just never thought the punishment would be so terrible and humiliating.

She hated being spanked; it made her feel small and

vulnerable. Was this how her sisters felt? They were spanked too, especially Corinne, who had a temper, but she'd never dare ask.

The belt dropped to the floor. Helene was tired from crying and her bottom was throbbing.

This was worse than the spanking he had given her the first time.

Her hand reached back towards her throbbing cheeks; maybe she should have just said goodbye to Zachary and finished her marriage goal by herself. But a part of her couldn't bear to say goodbye to Zachary. They had grown closer in these past few weeks, and besides, he was her best friend's brother, so how much longer could she possibly avoid him?

"Helene," Zachary croaked out. His voice sounded funny.

Helene didn't know what to say. Her heart was too broken. All she knew was that her relationship with Zachary had changed forever.

Chapter 9

A pair of ruby red cheeks stared back at Zachary, reminding him of what he had done. The once pale skin was now a splotchy red, swollen to the touch, with dark pink around the upper area of Helene's thighs.

Speaking of Helene, she was still draped over the expensive, uncomfortable chair, not daring to move for fear that the spanking would continue. Even though she had not moved from her space, her ass was trembling, making it appear all the more vulnerable.

He looked at the belt he was carrying and sighed. Zachary had gone too far and he knew it, but yet he couldn't bring himself to apologize. His stupid pride wouldn't let him. Helene choked on her sobs, which tugged at his heartstrings.

Zachary sighed; he needed to quiet Helene down. The last thing he needed was for the servants to hear her sobbing and come rushing in and find her spanked over his fine, antique chair.

He headed towards the back part of his bedroom,

grabbed a clean cloth, and then grabbed the pitcher to pour cold water on top of it. He then headed to the recently spanked girl and started cooling the hot cheeks with the cold, wet cloth.

Helene hissed when she felt the cool cloth on her bottom but didn't pull away; she just continued sobbing. Each sob only managed to break his heart more. He wanted to strangle himself for being so insensitive and cruel. Yes, Helene had deserved a spanking for barging in and risking both of their reputations, but she was an excited young girl who hadn't meant any harm. He shouldn't have belted her.

He looked at the poor little cheeks which would remain sore for days. Zachary wished he had some ointment on him, but he had run out.

His hand pulled down her skirts and petticoats but left her drawers pooled around her ankles. The less fabric she had around her rear end, the better. She could always keep her drawers here, or if she folded them neatly, she could probably place them inside the pocket of her dress.

"Helene, honey." Zachary tried to reach out to her, but Helene straightened up like a frightened rabbit. Her drawers tangled themselves against her ankles, causing her almost to trip, but Zachary managed to grip both of her wrists.

Helene's face rested on his chest for a mere moment before she pulled back. Her eyes were big and angry. He had never seen her so angry, especially at him. She raised her hand and slapped him across the face. Zachary had seen it coming but didn't pull back. Letting her slap him was the least he could do after he had belted her so harshly.

"I hate you," she hissed, "don't you dare speak to me again, or I will make you sorry."

"Helene, sweetheart, please."

Helene shook her head, refusing to let him speak. She stepped out of her drawers, opened his bedroom door, looked around to make sure there weren't any servants around and left.

Zachary gripped the drawers in his hand, feeling the softness of them. Some of her sweet scent still clung to them. Helene deserved an apology and he would give that to her, but she wouldn't listen to reason, at least not now.

He would let her calm down for a few weeks and then he would seek her forgiveness. It was the least he could do. Then, hopefully, Helene would forgive him and they could go back to the ways things were before he had lost his mind.

Until she became a Mrs. that is.

Helene could not stop crying as she roamed the streets of New York like an abandoned cat. It had gotten darker in the time between her running to Zachary and having her bottom blistered. The candles on the streetlamps were being lit by a father and young son. The two of them were covered in grease and had a curious look on their faces.

Helene couldn't blame them. It was odd that a young lady of her stature, who was inconveniently wearing an expensive dress, was seen wandering around the lonely streets of New York without even a maid to accompany her.

She hoped none of her mother's friends would see her; otherwise, they would surely tattle to her mother and she wouldn't be out of her room until she was thirty or she would find herself in the same situation as her sister Audrina had been. Married to a complete stranger.

The young woman shuddered at the thought. She wanted to marry, of course, but not a complete stranger. Besides, Dominic Darlington was rich and handsome, she doubted she would have the same luck.

Helene seemed to be having all types of bad luck lately.

When she thought about how excited she had been to receive the flowers from Carl Ashton, she wanted to slap herself. She had been so silly. Why would Zachary Easton care about who was sending her flowers? He had basically been guilted by her into accepting the position of flirting tutor. He was probably glad to be rid of her.

As she walked slowly, her thick skirts hit her sore bottom cheeks, reminding her of the thrashing her poor rump had received. It would be sore for days and the cold towel he had placed over the spanked cheeks had not helped at all.

She had never seen Zachary so angry before and while, yes, she probably deserved a little spanking for storming into his bachelor home with no thought for either of their reputations, she didn't think she deserved the belt for her misdeed.

Zachary had apologized, she would give him that, which was something he rarely did. Still, for such an offense, a simple apology would not work for Helene. A cold shoulder for at least a week was what he deserved.

She had told him that she hated him and never wanted to see him again. His hurt expression had pierced her conscience. She had never seen a man so heartbroken, with the exception of funerals.

But now that she had calmed down somewhat and was no longer crying, she realized that perhaps she might have been a bit harsh. Both she and Zachary had been unusually emotional tonight, and they both had said things that perhaps they hadn't meant.

Other women would have probably not looked in Zachary Easton's direction ever again, but the idea of never being near Zachary again made her physically ill, especially since he had been the one to make her a woman.

But he was also the one to blister your bottom, her inner voice silently scolded her. Perhaps she would think about it tomorrow, once her thoughts were no longer on the flowers she had received from Carl Ashton and her red bottom.

"Ow," she whimpered as she placed a hand on one sore buttock despite it being wildly inappropriate in the middle of the street. Being seen with her hands on her buttocks was the least of her worries.

It would seem she would have to pretend to be sick tomorrow as well, because the only thing she would want to do was lie on her belly while she felt sorry for herself. Besides having a pair of spanked cheeks, it wasn't hard to ignore the moisture which had gathered between her legs and was now dripping down her thighs.

While she might not have liked being belted, her body certainly did. If it wasn't for the heavy dress she was wearing, then her wetness might have been more noticeable.

She had brought up this predicament once or twice after Zachary had finished making love to her, but he had simply laughed at her, telling her she was being silly. Just because Helene was aware of her body's desire, didn't mean everyone else was.

Still, he had listened to her silliness and dried her off with a cloth before he dressed her after their lovemaking session. He hadn't this time, which was why she wasn't used to feeling the persistent wetness between her legs.

She supposed she could call for a bath, but the idea of sitting on her whipped bottom on a hard tub made her wince in pain. Helene would just have to go without a bath tonight, even though the water might help her bottom not feel as achy and sore.

Helene breathed a sigh of relief when she finally reached the Hollis residence. It was a miracle her parents had chosen today to go out and dine with their friends. If they had been in the house, Helene wouldn't be certain she would have been able to sneak in without being seen.

She shuddered at the thought of Mrs. Hollis finding out that she sneaked out to see an unmarried man and was seen wandering around the streets of New York alone.

Helene thought about going through the servants' entrance, but they would probably be having an early dinner since she was "sick". She wouldn't be able to come up with a decent explanation if she was caught.

Her hand slowly gripped the handle as she opened the door. A sigh of relief escaped her when she saw no one in the entryway. The girl hastily closed the door behind herself and hurried up the stairs.

Helene's heart didn't stop beating until she was safely in her own bedroom, away from prying eyes. She didn't bother grabbing her nightgown as she undressed. She would sleep in the nude tonight; it would certainly be more comfortable. Besides, she had gotten used to being naked in Zachary's arms.

Once she was nude, she turned her back to the tall mirror which stood in the corner of her bedroom, to stare at her rear end.

A pair of ruby red cheeks stared back at her, the color of the apples her mother liked having every morning for breakfast. The angry, dark pink marks of the belt could be seen from the upper part of her chubby cheeks down towards her thighs.

Small welts had also formed in the plumpest part of

her cheeks from where the belt had landed more than twice.

She let out a small cry when her fingers touched the welts. They stung more than the rest of her entire bottom. Sitting down was going to be a nightmare, for sure. Helene stood staring at her belted rump for the next ten minutes before she decided she was being silly.

Hopefully, her bottom would feel less painful the next morning.

Helene crawled into bed and hugged a pillow to her bare chest while she lay on her belly to make sure her rear end didn't touch the thick and stiff covers. Her heart felt heavy inside her chest while her eyes welled up with tears, thinking back to the last conversation she and Zachary had had.

Helene didn't know why, but the idea of never seeing him again utterly devastated her. She would take another spanking if it meant she would be able to lie in his arms once again.

She was a fool.

After spending an entire day in bed feeling sorry for herself and nursing her sore bottom, Helene realized she would never be able to pout in peace without her mother sending for a doctor. So, she allowed her maid to dress her and she took her place in the Hollises' sitting room in order to pretend to work on the same piece of embroidery that she had not been able to finish for the past few months, since Zachary had been keeping her busy.

Helene squirmed in her seat even though she tried not to. Her mother had already scolded her enough times about the matter. She had apologized, of course, but she couldn't tell Mrs. Hollis she was squirming because she had a spanked bottom.

She stared out the window. It was a beautiful May

morning, reminding her that summer was just around the corner. Many of the Hollises' family friends used the time to travel to Europe or spend time in their private houses in the country or near the seaside.

Not the Hollis family, however, both of her parents hated traveling and they seldom left the Hollis residence except to go to out-of-town weddings or to visit elderly relatives. It had driven Helene crazy when they were younger, but now she was glad they weren't going anywhere. Perhaps she was a fool, but leaving even for the summer would just make her miss Zachary more.

At least by staying in New York, she could pretend they were minutes away from being reunited. Helene sighed; no wonder her sisters thought she was a little fool. Maybe she should have just asked her parents to arrange a marriage to a stranger and she wouldn't have to deal with this right now.

"Is Kathleen coming to visit today?" her mother asked.

Kathleen usually visited every other day and Mrs. Hollis was used to dealing with their girlish squeals whenever they got together.

"I believe she's ill, Mother," she lied.

"Poor dear, it might be a late bout of influenza. They're rampant so close to the summer. I believe it's God's way of testing us. Miss Towers is suffering from it too, but have you seen the dresses she wears even when it's still daylight? I'm surprised she hadn't gotten sick sooner. If I was her mother, I would—"

Helene let her mother rant about Miss Towers. It was a nice distraction, especially since the only thing she could think of was the way Zachary's strong hands would trail up and down her legs whenever he undressed her.

"Mrs. Hollis, Miss Hollis, someone has come to call."

The Hollises' butler entered the room holding a small calling card on top of a silver tray.

Helene and her mother exchanged surprised looks. The only person who visited Helene was Kathleen, who didn't bother with a calling card, and usually, Mother's friends were let in immediately.

Helene wanted to snatch the calling card from the silver tray, but she forced herself to remain still and focus on her needlepointing. Mrs. Hollis' eyes scanned across the plain card. "Well, it seems Mr. Carl Ashton has come to visit. He's the one who sent you the bouquet of flowers two days ago, was he not?"

Of course, the servants kept her mother updated on everything. She was the lady of the house, after all.

Helene tried her best not to show her irritation as she forced a smile on her face. "Yes, he was."

She had ordered her lady's maid to throw her flowers out after her fight with Zachary because she couldn't bear to see them. It felt like they were staring at her in a mocking way.

Mrs. Hollis looked at her with approval. "Ashton's second son. A very good match and a very nice boy. It is encouraging that you caught his attention, Helene."

Helene let out a small, demure shrug. She strangely did not feel as excited as she had been when she had received the flowers. Mr. Ashton was a nice man, but he wasn't as witty as Zachary.

Stop thinking about him, she scolded the annoying voice in her head. *Zachary did not send you flowers nor did he call on you to apologize about his rudeness.*

After Mrs. Hollis instructed the butler to let Mr. Ashton in, Helene straightened in her seat even though it hurt her bottom. She plastered a fake smile on her face, silently hoping that Zachary was behind Carl, but of course, he wasn't.

The butler introduced Carl Ashton who was dressed in a navy-blue waistcoat with a matching jacket. His dark shoes had recently been polished and his blond hair reminded Helene of sunflowers.

He smiled at her and she realized he had very nice teeth with the exception of one of the lower ones, which was crooked.

Carl bowed his head before he went to kiss each of the ladies' hands. "Mrs. Hollis, Miss Hollis, it is a pleasure to see both of your lovely smiles on this fine morning."

Mrs. Hollis actually blushed, which was almost comical. Helene had never seen her mother blush before. He turned to Helene, and she moved to the side so he didn't sit on her wide skirt. Since company was present, she had to sit straight up, putting unnecessary pressure on her still sore bottom.

"Thank you."

"Would you care for some tea? Cookies?" Helene asked awkwardly. She had never had to act like a hostess. That was usually her mother or her sisters' job.

Carl nodded politely.

After she rang for tea and cookies, her mother told them she had an important letter to finish writing at the desk across the sitting room, giving them a sense of privacy even though she could obviously hear everything.

"Thank you for the flowers," Helene said, once the maid brought over the tea and cookies. "I'm sorry I did not send a thank you card. I've been feeling a bit under the weather."

Carl cleared his throat. "Of course, Miss Hollis, I understand. Did you enjoy them?"

"Very much so. Did you pick them out?"

"The florist did."

"Well, she did a very fine job."

The conversation was stiff, at best. Helene had more interesting conversations with her maid. For the next thirty minutes, they talked about more mundane topics, like the weather, the latest ball both of them had been invited to, and oddly enough, horses.

"Thank you so much for your kind hospitality, Miss Hollis." Carl stood up.

"Thank you for visiting. It was a pleasure."

Carl looked pleased by the compliment. "May I see you again, Miss Hollis? I would like to take you on a carriage ride through the park. If your mother permits it, that is."

The idea of going on a carriage ride with her mother as chaperone sounded dreadful to Helene, especially since she had spent so much time being in the same room alone with Zachary. Spending time with men was much more pleasurable with no mothers present, that was for sure.

But she needed to stop thinking about Zachary. He had told her from the start that he was not the marrying kind, and besides, any form of contact had surely been cut off, at least for a while, after their screaming match. Carl Ashton was a nice young man; he wouldn't be the most horrid of husbands. After the babies came, they would probably never spend time together, just like her own mother and father.

She found herself saying, "If Mother permits it, a carriage ride sounds lovely."

Six Months Later, November 1852

"Welcome back, sir," Zachary's butler greeted him as he opened the door for him. Zachary stomped inside, not caring that he was covering the carpet with mud. He knew the maids would clean it up, and honestly, he was in such a foul mood that he didn't care if he came off as rude.

He had been in an awful mood ever since he and Helene had parted ways. So much so that he had two maids quit as well as his former valet because they couldn't take his foul mood anymore.

All of this because of a little redheaded minx who had nothing better to do than mess with his head even if he hadn't heard a peep from her in the last six months. After spanking her, he had assumed they would spend some time apart until both of their heads had cooled. He hadn't imagined it would be for half a year. It was nearly Christmas, for God's sake! Weren't people supposed to be more forgiving around the holidays?

Zachary had sent her flowers and chocolates during the first few weeks after their argument, but when both of those attempts had gone unanswered, he had left her alone with the hope she would seek him out.

She didn't.

She also wasn't moping at home like he had been, either. According to Kathleen, she was at a ball every week with men arguing for the chance to write their names on her dance card, so she wasn't exactly suffering. Helene had gotten over her shyness and was apparently winning over men with her wit. Something she used to reserve only for him.

Kathleen had begged him to be her chaperone for the many balls she was invited to so she didn't have to bring their father along. He had refused. It was clear Helene didn't want to see him and he didn't want to see men making fools of themselves.

Helene was choosing to ignore him, which was fine for him. He wasn't one to beg for scraps of affections anyhow.

Still, it hurt that she wasn't acknowledging him even a little.

"Sir?"

"What?"

"You have received an invitation. Shall I put it with the rest of the correspondence?"

"No, give it to me."

Zachary received a creamy white envelope made of fine, thick paper. It was sealed with navy blue wax which had a curly H in the center. He tore it immediately and scanned the invitation.

It didn't say much, just that Mr. and Mrs. Hollis were inviting him to a ball thrown in honor of their daughter, Miss Helene Hollis. The Hollis family did not throw many balls so this was surprising.

At the bottom of the invitation, there was the following message written in Helene's curly handwriting, *Please come. I want you to see that your work has come to fruition. Yours truly, Helene.*

Chapter 10

The road leading to the Hollises' large townhouse was filled with carriages, to the point that not even Zachary's own driver could go through. Eventually, he told his driver he would just get out in the middle of the road and for him to pick him up in two hours.

That should be enough time to talk to Helene. It was a ball, not a formal dinner, so he would be able to get more than a few minutes alone with her even if she was the one celebrating tonight for some unknown reason. The Hollises' family home had many nooks and crannies; he could quite comfortably hide the redhead.

Loud grumbling was coming from the nearby carriages, obviously the results of impatient guests waiting to be let out.

He frowned as he looked at the invitation in his hand. He had opened it and closed it so many times, it was crooked with wear. Why was the Hollis family celebrating Helene tonight? He couldn't help but wonder. Helene had always been considered the bizarre, ugly duckling compared to Corinne and Audrina.

Zachary hoped they weren't sending her off to finishing school in Europe like some New York best families did, in the hope that their daughters would snag a European husband. Given that Corinne and Audrina now lived in Europe, he had no doubt her sisters had encouraged her to spend some time in London. He could chase after her, of course, but he would risk his father murdering him. The older man wanted to retire and he had told him he had given him plenty of time to sow his wild oats.

There was no other explanation. That must be what this ball was about, to celebrate her departure. Zachary's stomach churned with dread and he scolded himself internally for not apologizing earlier.

He handed the invitation to the Hollises' butler who simply raised an eyebrow when he saw how messy it was. "Mr. Zachary Easton."

A few friendly faces greeted him as Zachary forced himself to stop and make polite conversations when what he really wanted was to search for Helene. After talking to the elderly Mrs. Robinson for what felt like hours, he found himself asking, "Have you seen Mr. and Mrs. Hollis and Miss Hollis? I would like to pay my respects to the hosts."

Mrs. Robinson nodded as she pointed to the center of the Hollises' ballroom, where Helene and her parents stood. Helene's father looked intoxicated even though it was barely nine in the evening, while Mrs. Hollis looked pleased, something which she rarely was.

Helene stood beside her parents like a dutiful daughter, wearing a green and cream ballroom dress with dyed, gold-colored lace. Her red hair had been braided before being put into a high bun, showing off her smooth, pale neck.

She was smiling, but it was a nervous smile, like when

she had first started visiting him to teach her about the rules of the marriage bed. Next to her was none other than Carl Ashton, looking rather dapper in new clothes with his hair slicked back. He was so stiff, he almost looked like a footman.

But despite his stiff demeanor, Zachary saw something else in his facial expression—pride. Something he rarely saw. He was the youngest son in his family, only mildly attractive, and irrelevant in regards to New York society, who had bigger fish to worry about. Beside Carl, were his stiff-looking parents who seemed unnerved by all of the attention they were receiving.

His stomach suddenly dropped while perspiration clung to his forehead. There was only one reason why Ashton would have such a prideful expression on his face and it didn't lead to anything good in Zachary's book.

It had been six months since he had spoken to Helene, and a lot could have happened since then. But if something had happened, surely, his sister would have told him, right? Unless Helene had begged Kathleen to keep whatever her family was about to share a secret.

She wouldn't be so cruel as to let him come to this party not knowing about what would occur, right? Helene's note had been obscure at best, but he had thought nothing of it, thinking the girl was just being difficult again. Maybe he should have paid more attention.

How bad would it make him look if he took Helene and dragged her to the nearest coat closet or parlor and spoke with her?

His father would be furious while his sister would be embarrassed. Until his sister was properly married off, he needed to keep his mouth shut.

Zachary stood beside an elderly widow who seemed to be having a one-sided conversation while he only half-listened. It took all his willpower to stay with his feet firmly planted on the ground.

Instead, he focused on Helene's pale neck which was adorned with an emerald and diamond necklace. Just a few months ago, Zachary had been buried against her willowy neck, breathing her sweet lily and jasmine scented perfume. He had been a fool to let her go.

Now, he was paying the price for his foolish pride.

When he was a little boy, his mother had often warned him that pride was the most terrible of sins. He wished he had listened. However, it was too late now.

Mr. Hollis cleared his throat, causing the group of thirteen musicians behind him to stop playing. It seemed like the entirety of New York's social circle was in attendance in the Hollises' ballroom tonight, waiting for some surprise revelation.

The Hollis family rarely threw balls, mainly because of Mrs. Hollis' shrewish nature, but also because the reputation of the family had dwindled when their eldest daughter had been caught being sexually intimate with a British gentlemen and then their middle daughter returned to New York suddenly married.

Their reputation had never recovered since then. Whatever the news was, it had to be big, which didn't make him feel better.

"Thank you all for attending this little soiree; our family is grateful." Mr. Hollis beamed as he squeezed his wife's hand. "I am very happy to be surrounded by so many people who wish us well."

They're praying for your downfall, old man, so they can take your place, Zachary replied nastily in his head.

"I am happy to announce that this is not just a simple party, it is actually the opportunity to celebrate with our closest friends the engagement of my youngest daughter, Miss Helene Hollis, to Mr. Carl Ashton."

The room burst into applause while Zachary had to grasp the shoulder of a wandering footman to keep from fainting. Everything around him was spinning and he had the sensation of wanting to vomit despite his stomach being empty.

"Sir, are you okay?" the footman asked. He couldn't be more than seventeen and didn't know how complicated love was or the headaches it caused.

"I'm perfectly all right. I apologize," he forced himself to say as he looked back at the redhead who was receiving congratulating hugs from her fussy aunts.

She still hadn't realized he was mere feet away. Her pretty head was wrapped around the thoughts of engagements, babies, and wedding planning.

Helene Hollis would go on living life as Mrs. Ashton, while he was doomed to wander the streets of New York only thinking of her and her bright red hair. It all made sense now. How could he be so foolish?

He loved Helene Hollis.

More than he had ever loved any woman.

It was the reason why he hadn't been able to stomach food in six months, how all his thoughts drifted to the redhead, and how he had stupidly thought she would wait for him like he had.

Zachary had been so stupid. Of course, she would not wait. She had told him marriage was the goal and she had found someone who would marry her.

"Mr. Easton."

Zachary looked up and saw Helene looking at him demurely. He must have walked towards her and Carl without noticing. Thankfully, Carl seemed oblivious to the exchange.

Helene had a tiny smile on her face. All the anger from the previous months seemed to have diminished and they were standing still, like polite acquaintances. Zachary hated it.

"Congratulations," he managed to choke out as he looked at the dainty gold ring with the diamond in the center. He would have gotten her a much bigger ring. "Are you happy?"

She nodded, letting him know their argument from months prior was long forgotten. "Very much so." She paused, then lowered her voice. "I hope you're happy too, Zachary."

Zachary wanted to do nothing more than whisk her away and lock her in his bedroom, but he couldn't. He had been selfish enough that he had already lost her and needed to let her go.

"Easton, you came to celebrate." Carl patted him on the shoulder. Suddenly, he hated the stupid grin on his face as if he'd won some sort of prize.

Zachary gave him a curt nod. He suddenly felt hot and itchy, as if he needed to get out of here. *Now.* The sounds of people congratulating Helene and Carl were driving him insane.

"Congratulations," he managed to say again before he slipped out of the ballroom.

His beating heart calmed down somewhat once he was in the Hollises' entryway. He should leave to go wallow in self-pity, but he couldn't force his feet to move to the entrance. Instead, he found himself going into the Hollises' library where Helene's father was handing out cigars to celebrate his daughter's engagement to all of the men.

"Easton, for you." Mr. Hollis handed him a thick cigar. "For you, we're celebrating!"

Zachary accepted the cigar without a reply. The only

way he was going to be able to survive this dreadful night was to get painfully drunk and to smoke all evening.

Helene Hollis was engaged and he only had himself to blame.

He should have never participated in her little plan. But then again, he never thought he was going to be the one being hurt.

An hour later, Zachary was half-listening to Peter Ellis as he droned on about his latest business acquisition, while trying to fight the sleepiness. The last thing he needed was to pass out in the Hollises' library. Mr. Hollis had left to go dance with the bride-to-be, even though he could barely stand on his two feet.

The room suddenly erupted in manly cheers. He sat up in confusion and saw that Carl had come in looking like a proud rooster with his chest puffed up, even though he had done nothing noteworthy other than get engaged to the most beautiful girl in all of New York.

The men congratulated and teased him about his upcoming wedding while Zachary ignored him. Carl Ashton, more than likely, would not satisfy his wife in the marriage bed. While he was making love to Helene, she would probably be thinking about him and all the times he'd managed to make her scream in pleasure.

He was surprised he had grown bitter in such a short amount of time.

A man whose name Zachary had forgotten elbowed Carl in the ribs. "Are you excited about your wedding night, Ashton?"

Carl grinned like an idiot. "I can't think of anything else but having Helene Hollis on all fours grunting like a pig while every part of her bounces while I'm having my way with her. I am going to tear into her cunny. I can't wait to watch her bleed—"

Zachary did not let him finish his sentence because he stood up and started pummeling him, burying his fist against his nose and mouth. His knuckles hurt and he heard the crack of bone which was more than likely Carl's nose.

He ignored the noises around him; the only thing Zachary felt at that moment was pure, unfiltered rage at many things. Carl speaking of Helene as if she were a cow ready for breeding instead of giving her the respect she deserved, Helene accepting the proposal of another man, and him being cowardly enough not to apologize and pushing Helene into the arms of a useless man.

Someone tried to pull Zachary back, but he was too far gone, his anger giving him the rage he did not know he had. He felt his hands being covered with blood while Carl groaned in pain underneath him.

Zachary felt a sharp blow to his stomach which distracted him enough to stop punching him. Carl let out a scream like a wild animal as he pushed Zachary away from him, hitting Zachary's head harshly against one of the tables.

None of them attempted to pull them apart, either fascinated by the spectacle or deciding it was pointless to intervene. Neither of them were talking; they were just a tumble of legs and arms, each of them fighting for the chance to injure a part of the other.

They found themselves tumbling into the ballroom which was only a few feet away. The entire room fell silent when they stumbled in with their faces bruised and their clothes unkempt.

Helene, who had been gossiping with Kathleen, gaped as if she couldn't believe the scene in front of her. She turned pale as if she could sense what was coming. It would be a miracle if both his and Helene's reputations went undamaged, but it was too late for that now.

Mrs. Hollis looked like she wanted to throw both of them in jail. Mr. Hollis and Zachary's own father, Mr. Easton, pulled them apart.

Mr. Easton's face was red with anger. "What in the devil is going on, Zachary? What are you two doing?"

Zachary ignored his father, ignored Carl, who looked like he was going to faint, and ignored Mr. Hollis, who seemed to be the only one to have grasped what had occurred.

Zachary needed to do this in front of everyone. He couldn't hold it in any longer; perhaps there was still time to make things right. To make Helene see he was the only man for her. The man who should be her husband.

If she wanted him to go on his hands and knees and beg for her forgiveness, he would, as long as she broke off her engagement to Carl.

"Helene!" Zachary croaked out. "I know you are bound to another, but I want to marry you. Please accept my humble proposal of matrimony."

One hundred and twenty-two pairs of eyes turned to stare at Helene, who was blushing deeply. He couldn't stand the look on her pretty face. She was wearing a look he hated seeing in women. Pity.

Helene took a step forward and whispered the most hurtful words that she could have ever uttered, "I think you should go home, Mr. Easton."

Chapter 11

"Drink," Kathleen scolded her older brother as she lifted a glass of water towards his parched lips. "You're still drunk."

Zachary forced himself to drink the liquid even if his stomach rumbled in protest. The last thing he wanted was to vomit on his sister. It would be the icing on a terribly long day.

After he had been kicked out of the Hollises' residence, he had returned to his bachelor home and drunk a large amount of liquor while telling his servants not to disturb him.

"Does Father know you're here?"

She nodded, looking at him with pity. "He's furious. He thinks you made a fool of yourself. He's with Mr. Hollis and the elder Mr. Ashton right now, asking for their forgiveness. He's telling them you had too much to drink and this was an act of foolishness and should not reflect on Miss Hollis in any way."

He nodded. So, the wedding was still going to happen.

She cocked her head to the side. "You love Helene, don't you? How long has your little affair been going on?"

Zachary looked at her in surprise while his sister laughed.

"I might be young, Zach, but I am not a complete idiot. I've seen the little looks you give each other. Helene was acting weird for a time, always asking or looking for you. It stopped when she started courting Carl."

"It wasn't an affair. It was…" Affair was such an ugly word, but he didn't know what else to call what transpired between them. "It doesn't matter, but you're right. I do love her. I'm not sure she feels the same way. Do you think she'll cancel her engagement to Carl?"

Kathleen shook her head sadly as she patted his knee. "I do not think so. I'm sorry, Zachary."

He rested his head against her shoulder, trying not to let his sadness show. "It might be for the best."

"Don't frown, dear, it makes you look unattractive," Mrs. Hollis scolded gently during teatime a few days after the "incident" as everyone in New York, even the servants, called it. Her mother had barely gotten out of bed today to join Helene for tea and sewing. With the way Mrs. Hollis was acting, you would think she was the one who had been humiliated at her own engagement party.

Surprisingly, Helene was not angry. Instead, she was simply confused, unsure of what to do. She hadn't heard from either Carl or Zachary in days, not even Kathleen, which was giving her plenty of time to think.

"What's on your mind, dear?"

"Many things, Mother," Helene confessed. She didn't have her sisters with her, so her mother would have to do.

"I'm not sure if I should continue to plan my wedding to Mr. Ashton."

"Is it because of Mr. Easton's ridiculous proposal?" she inquired. "Are you sweet on him? He must have made quite an impression when he took you on that walk in the park."

Helene blushed. Of course, her mother thought she and Zachary had only interacted once. When he took her to the park and at the occasional ball.

"He's a nice man," Helene said quietly as she fiddled with her fingers. "He's also Kathleen's brother and we played together when we were children."

"That's hardly a reason to marry the man. Though I suppose you could do worse, and at least, he hasn't been seducing every whore in a five-mile radius like that horrid Harry Michaelson." Mrs. Hollis cocked her head to the side. "Is there something you're not telling me, Helene?"

"Of course not, Mother."

"Because if there is, you must tell me."

"Nothing has happened between me and Mr. Easton, Mother."

"I do not want another scandal, Corinne and Audrina have given me plenty of worries. I thought you, at least, would let my heart rest when it came to your marriage."

"Believe me, there will not be a scandal." She paused, thinking of the ball. "At least not more than you already witnessed."

"Well, good." Mrs. Hollis hesitated. "Though you still look worried, dear. I do not want you to leave Mr. Ashton at the altar only for you to run into that fool's arms."

"The wedding is still months away," she pointed out. "And I'm not worried, exactly, I just don't want to make the wrong choice."

Mrs. Hollis looked perplexed at the question. "You

should be grateful that you have a choice. Though, if you ask me, being given choices has made you girls vain and silly."

Helene had forgotten her own parents had an arranged marriage. They hadn't been unhappy per se, but she didn't notice any hatred or happiness between them. Mr. and Mrs. Hollis seemed to exist apart even if they had lived in the same house for twenty-seven years, only getting together for dinner. They hadn't even shared the same bedroom since Helene had been born and Mrs. Hollis had been told she was too old to bear any more children.

A distant marriage seemed to her sadder than an unhappy one. It would be like endless walking, but without reaching a clear destination.

Then she thought about her sisters' marriages. Corinne had been forced to marry after being astute enough to seduce half of New York's most eligible bachelors—and a few married men—and Audrina had had an arranged marriage to Dominic Darlington. They had both been unhappy at first, but now they were content, with children of their own.

Would that happen to Helene? Maybe she should have allowed her parents to choose a suitor for her, then she would have been able to avoid this headache.

Helene sighed as she rested her chin against the palm of her hand. "I just don't want to be unhappy, Mother, is that too much to ask?"

"You sound like a spoiled child."

"Then who do you think I should marry?"

Mrs. Hollis paused, surprised she had been asked this question. "Well, people are already gossiping because of the spectacle your gentlemen made. I believe giving them something else to talk about wouldn't cause much harm.

Given the choice, I think you should marry Zachary Easton."

"Really? Why?" Helene was surprised by her mother's answer. She thought she would have her pick Carl Ashton so they could avoid another scandal.

Mrs. Hollis looked at her as if the answer should have been obvious. "Well, Zachary Easton is the better match between the two. Though, I still believe you could have chosen better. He is the only son of old man Easton, so he will inherit his fortune. He is not bad looking, does not drink heavily, and is not a violent man. He is more mature than he was when he was a young man when he had an itchy foot for traveling. I suspect he will make a fine husband. Carl Ashton is a nice boy, but that's all he is—a boy. You need a grown, well-adjusted man. Besides, Carl is not the first son, he will receive a pittance compared to the eldest brother. You might be my third daughter, Helene, but you are still a Hollis girl. If your sisters can make brilliant matches, I have no doubt you can as well. You can do far worse than Zachary Easton."

Helene laughed for the first time in days, feeling the tension leave her body. Perhaps it was because she finally had an answer and she actually had her parents' approval despite her worries.

"Oh, Mother, you are always so practical."

"Well, yes, dear, one has to be if they want to survive as a woman in our world."

Helene called for Carl Ashton the following afternoon. The last thing she needed was for her mother to regret her advice or for her father to throw a fit. Mother had protested it was unladylike for an unmarried woman to send a message to a bachelor, but they were still technically engaged and Helene was too impatient to wait any longer.

Carl had not visited her since their engagement ball.

Probably because he was too embarrassed that Zachary had beaten him to a bloody pulp. Helene had no choice but to call for him herself.

Helene felt a bit silly. What if she broke off her engagement with Carl and it turned out Zachary had just proposed to her in a fit of rage? It wasn't like Zachary had contacted her, either. With her luck, Helene might end up having no fiancé.

She dried her sweaty hands against her pale-yellow dress as she paced around the sitting room waiting for Carl. She had asked for him to come at three before she and her mother had tea. She supposed an hour would be plenty of time to break off an engagement. Helene doubted either of them would be particularly heartbroken. They hadn't talked much besides about the weather and other polite topics, nothing like she and Zachary.

Helene had hoped they would have been more open with each other after their wedding. Thankfully, that was no longer a concern for her.

"Mr. Carl Ashton."

Carl stepped into the room looking like a pouty child. Bruises still covered his pale face from where Zachary had struck him. Helene could hardly believe two men had fought over her. She never thought that would happen.

"Miss Hollis." He pressed his lips against the back of her hand. "I came as soon as I got your message. I must say I was surprised to have received it."

"Thank you so much for coming." Helene suddenly felt very nervous. "Please, sit. I sent for tea, unless you prefer coffee?"

"Tea is fine, though with the pain I am in, I wouldn't say no to a whisky." He rubbed his sore bottom lip. "I must say I never expected Zachary Easton to be such a brute. I should have called for the police to have him arrested, but my father wouldn't hear of it. He said it would be an embarrassment."

Carl blushed when he realized he was going off on a tangent. "Is there something you want to discuss, sweetest? Are you worried about the bruising? Do not worry, my doctor promises they will be gone just in time for the wedding."

"That is what I wanted to discuss with you, the wedding." She wiped her sweaty palms against her dress, suddenly hating that her mother had chosen this opportunity to stop meddling and give her and Carl privacy. She removed her engagement ring which had belonged to Carl's grandmother. "I'm afraid I can no longer marry you. I'm sorry. Please forgive me."

Carl's jaw tightened as he took the ring. "Is it because of the fight? It was not a fair fight, Zachary did things no gentleman would ever dream of doing."

"It's not because of the fight. I realized we do not belong together as a married couple should."

"Why did you realize it now and not in the six months we were courting?"

Helene blushed. She couldn't tell him it was because she was in love with the man who beat him and who had shared her bed for months. "I am truly sorry. I did not mean to cause you any harm."

Carl laughed coldly as he stood up. "You will not get another proposal if you go through with it. Society will say that you are ruined and that's why the wedding did not go through. No one wants to marry a woman who broke off a proper engagement. You make me seem like a fool."

"No one likes a jilted man, either," Helene spoke up quietly. "People might wonder if you did anything wrong or had any secrets which had come to light. Mr. Ashton, despite your disapproval, I am still a Hollis girl and my word matters just as much as yours. Maybe more."

"Perhaps the Hollis family at one point was well regarded, but it stopped when Corinne was known to warm the bed of every stranger and Audrina came back from her trip suddenly married. You can add yourself to the list of failures otherwise known as the Hollis sisters. Your parents must be proud."

Helene smiled coldly at him as she arched her head to the door. "I will give them your message, Mr. Ashton. Now please leave and never come back."

Chapter 12

Helene opened her eyes when she heard swearing. She wrapped the covers around herself, trying not to feel frightened. Who could have uttered those terrible words? Should she scream? Cry for help?

She flinched when the swearing became louder and she heard a branch hit one of her windows.

Her body relaxed only a bit when she recognized who it was. Zachary.

Helene didn't have a clock in her bedroom because she thought they were too noisy, but it must be after midnight. What could he possibly be doing here?

Curiosity got the best of her and Helene found herself crawling out of bed and heading to the window, not bothering to put on a shawl or a robe. The man had seen her naked for goodness' sake.

Helene opened the window, and as soon as she did, she saw a large male hand followed by a large body which was covered in leaves. Zachary appeared red-faced and annoyed, with a small branch in his dark hair.

Helene giggled as she helped him into her room.

Zachary pressed a hand against his clothing. "It's not funny, Hel. The stupid tree outside almost knocked me down. Thankfully, I don't have to explain to your family why I ended up with a broken leg outside your window." Helene giggled at the thought. Zachary looked exhausted. "Don't laugh, brat, it's not funny."

"If I laugh, will you spank me?"

Zachary had the decency to look embarrassed. "I shouldn't have spanked you in anger a few months ago. I apologize. I acted like a brute and I deserved your anger and everything else."

Helene nodded calmly. "Thank you for apologizing. I should probably think before acting. You were right, reputation does matter, even if we don't think so. New York, especially, can be quite unforgiving." She paused suddenly, looking somber. "Why are you here, Zach?"

He swallowed, looking unsure for the first time since she had met him. "Kathleen told me you broke off your engagement to Carl."

She nodded. "And?"

"Why did you? Did our spectacle seal things for you?"

Helene shook her head. "No. I imagined the years flying past me and I didn't like what I saw. Ending my life being known as Mrs. Carl Ashton." She bit her lower lip. "Especially when I couldn't stop thinking of you."

Zachary perked up. "Really?"

She nodded. "When I thought about my wedding, trips, and babies, the only person I could think of being by my side was you, Zachary." Her eyes twinkled. "Of course, your fight for my honor helped a little."

"Was Carl upset?" he asked carefully, trying to hide the smile on his face. A broken engagement when they had just had a party to celebrate was almost unheard of, but he would defend Helene to the bitter end if anyone so much as gave her a dirty look.

"He was. He said I humiliated him before the wedding and everyone would think him a fool."

"He is a fool."

Helene rolled her eyes. "But he won't say anything other than the engagement was mutually canceled on both of our ends."

"How can you be so sure?"

"Because a broken engagement so soon after an engagement party looks just as bad for him as it does for me." She squeezed both of his hands gently. "Carl knows he is not the most eligible bachelor. After the news breaks out, people might wonder why the engagement was broken off and they might think twice before introducing their unmarried daughters to him. So, no, I am not worried about Carl."

"If he does anything to hurt you—" he warned.

"I know you will take care of him." Helene laughed. "I don't know what caused you to lose control like you did at the party, but thank you for defending my honor."

"He was insulting you. That is all you need to know."

"Because I am not as pretty as my sisters. I suppose most men see me as a consolation prize. I suppose it's better to have Helene Hollis than to not have any Hollis sister at all." She did not say the words with pain, but with acceptance. How many had made her feel like the lesser Hollis sister because she was not dark-haired?

Zachary landed three swats on her bottom harshly, causing her to yelp out in pain. She whacked him on the arm before she started rubbing her bottom. "What was that for?"

"For insulting yourself in my presence. You are beautiful, Helene, never forget that. If I hear you diminishing your beauty, you will find yourself over my lap, and this time I will not apologize."

Helene rolled her eyes but didn't argue. A pink blush coated her cheeks.

Zachary removed the scowl from his face, and his eyes settled on her puckered nipples which were visible in her thin nightgown. "So, Miss Hollis, are you on the market again?"

She nodded, an amused look on her face. "Yes, I am, and I'm terribly cold." She wrapped her arms around his neck, standing on her tippy toes as she did so. Helene felt a familiar throbbing between her legs. She had forgotten how much she missed it. "Will you warm me up?"

Zachary seemed surprised by her boldness until he cupped her quim in his large hand and squeezed it. "Whatever my lady desires."

He made love to her until the early hours of the morning when the sun's rays were just beginning to peek in through Helene's window. Helene had lost count of how many times she tried to muzzle her screams as Zachary entered her. He had even finished inside her this time, and for once, neither of them were worried about pregnancy.

Helene was still surprised by how nice his warm seed felt inside her. No wonder Corinne and Audrina had gotten pregnant soon after their weddings.

"I should get going," Zachary said apologetically.

"You should," she declared.

"I have something I must ask you."

"What is it?"

"Marry me," he declared, a lopsided smile on his handsome face. "I do not have a ring with me, but I promise I will purchase you the prettiest ring in all of New York if you say yes."

Helene laughed as she kissed him. "I would have married you without a ring. I am just happy you finally asked me."

Chapter 13

The weeks flew by and before Helene Hollis knew it, it was a week before her appointed wedding date. Helene had been afraid the date would never come, or worse, that something tragic would happen which would separate her and Zachary from being lawfully wed.

Her mother and Kathleen thought she was being silly and needed to stop reading so many romance novels, but at least her future husband was amused even if he did tease her about her worries.

In just a week, she would be Mrs. Zachary Easton and Helene could hardly believe it herself. She had to stare at her engagement ring multiple times throughout the day to make sure that she was still engaged.

To think she would marry the man who said he would never marry and who promised to choose her husband for her.

If it had been up to her, she would have married Zachary in her old church dress. After spending months seeking his company and being in his arms, it felt weird not being around him anymore. When they were in public, they had to maintain their distance even if they were engaged, and worst of all, her mother was keeping a stricter eye on her, so she couldn't even sneak out in her maid's outfit like she so often had.

Zachary didn't want a large or elaborate wedding, either, but they were both suffering through to please their meddling parents. Helene was the last Hollis daughter to get married and Zachary was Mr. Easton's only son.

"I still feel like I'm forgetting something," Mrs. Hollis said with a grimace on her smooth face.

Helene placed a hand on her mother's thin shoulder as she scowled at the flower arrangements one of the maids had put out. "Everything is done, Mother." The Easton family was coming by for dinner tonight. It would be their last time together before Zachary and Helene were married.

"That's why I want everything to be perfect," Mrs. Hollis sniffed. "You don't seem to have a care in the world. This is your wedding, in case you've forgotten."

"I know." Helene shrugged, not bothered by her mother's sharp tone. She knew it was stress relating to the wedding. Besides, she would be out of the house soon and she wouldn't have to deal with her mother's constant worrying. "But I just want to be married to Zachary. I don't care if I marry him in our living room."

Mrs. Hollis seemed horrified at the thought. Without a look back, she left Helene standing there, probably on her way to yell at some poor maids.

Helene sighed as she looked at the large portrait leading up the stairs. It was a portrait of her and her two sisters the year of Corinne's debut. Corinne was eighteen, dressed in a white gown, wearing a haughty expression. Audrina was standing next to her, looking quite young next to Corinne's smirking face, while Helene was sitting on the floor next to Corinne's full skirts at just ten years old.

She wished her sisters and her husbands could make the journey, but even though the wedding invitations had been sent urgently, it was still a long trip from Europe.

"Miss Hollis?"

Helene looked up and saw her lady's maid at the top of the stairs with tears in her eyes. No doubt her mother had yelled at her again. "Yes?"

"Your mother wants me to do your hair this evening the way she likes. The Easton family will be coming soon and you still need to bathe and get dressed. Perhaps it's time that we get started."

Helene sighed; she didn't particularly like being poked and prodded for hours, but her mother was already tense enough. She could give her this at least. She wouldn't be under her thumb for very long and the last thing she needed was for her and her maid to get yelled at. "Lead the way."

Two hours later, Helene and the rest of the Hollis family were in the sitting room waiting for the Easton family. Helene's red hair was pulled back in a tight bun, which was quite honestly cutting circulation to her head, and in her favorite navy-blue dress she had worn when she saw Zachary for the first time after he returned to New York.

Mrs. Hollis hated the dress because it showed off too much of her bosom, but Helene loved it and she knew it would make Zachary smile.

"Mr. Easton, Mr. Zachary Easton, Miss Easton," the Hollis butler announced.

The three members of the Easton family entered the sitting room dressed in their evening best. Zachary winked at Helene when he noticed her staring at him. To think he was going to be her husband in a matter of days.

Once pleasantries were over, Mrs. Hollis invited them into the dining room. Helene was surrounded by plates of good food and wine, but while everyone else talked about the wedding or upcoming trips, the only thing Helene wanted to do was grip Zachary by his evening jacket and kiss him until both of their lips were bruised.

Helene had been hoping to have a moment of privacy with her fiancé, but alas, that was not the case. The men secluded themselves in the Hollises' library to drink brandy, smoke cigars, and rant about politics.

Meanwhile, Mrs. Hollis was making Kathleen and Helene miserable by complaining non-stop about wedding details over coffee.

After what seemed like hours, Mr. Easton stepped back into the sitting room. Both he and her father looked terribly drunk. "We must get going, it's getting late." He kissed the back of Mrs. Hollis' hand noisily, causing the poor woman to become embarrassed. "Thank you for a lovely dinner, Mrs. Hollis, Miss Hollis. I'm thankful two great families like ours will be united. I'll send my Kathleen to you on the day of the wedding so the bride and maid-of-honor can arrive together. Until the wedding."

Helene bit her lip as she looked at Zachary who was holding his father upright. No, they couldn't leave yet!

"Zach!" she cried out, causing the Easton family to look at her.

Her mother glared as she often did, probably afraid Helene was going to ruin things a week before her wedding. Her father was too intoxicated to notice she was behaving rudely.

Helene flushed bright red but stood her ground. "May I please speak with you before you depart?"

Mrs. Hollis shook her head. "It's inappropriate."

"The children will be married in a week, one conversation won't hurt." The elder Mr. Easton burped.

Mrs. Hollis sighed reluctantly. "In the hall where I can still see you. Make it quick,

Helene. You won't see Mr. Easton until the wedding on Saturday."

Helene nodded, silently thanking her mother for her rare generosity. Helene and Zachary met by the large staircase. Zachary gripped her hand which was sweating through her gloves.

"What did you need to tell me, Hel?"

"Nothing," she admitted. "I just needed to speak to you about anything really. I am not used to our parents meddling in our every conversation."

Zachary laughed, his blue eyes twinkling. "My, Miss Hollis, do you miss being unladylike and sneaking around with me at all hours? What part do you miss the most? My cunning smile? Me whispering sweet things in your delicate ears? Making love to me?"

Helene rolled her eyes. "You do know vanity is quite a sin?"

"I am aware, though you seem to enjoy it." He placed a hand underneath her chin and forced her to stare at him. "Chin up, Hel. In a week, you will be Mrs. Easton and you never have to leave my bed."

Helene smiled. "I'm looking forward to it."

"Good. Now, let me leave before my future mother-in-law faints."

It was the evening before her wedding, and Helene couldn't recall the last time she had felt so nervous. Her mother had sent her to bed at eight so that she could be well-rested, but the only thing she had accomplished was to toss and turn for hours.

Questions plagued her mind. Would she be a happy bride? Would she and Zachary share the same passionate love twenty years from now? Would she be as happy as her sisters?

She heard a loud creak coming from the window near her vanity and she sat up. Could it be a burglar?

Helene trembled when she saw a large hand on her small balcony followed by a groan. She had been about to yell for help when she recognized the brown hair. Zachary.

"You scared me," she scolded him as her heart finally stopped beating rapidly inside her chest.

"You shouldn't be leaving the windows open," he scolded.

She gave a tiny shrug of her shoulders. "I was hot. What are you doing here?"

He didn't answer right away; instead, he leaned over and kissed her while she was still sitting on the bed on her knees. His kiss felt warm and sweet and she wished she could taste it forever.

"I've missed you," he murmured as he pressed a thumb against her lower lip. "This week without you has been hell."

Her heart fluttered as she pressed her face against his thumb. "Really?"

He laughed. "I think you're fishing for compliments, Miss Hollis."

Helene gave a little shrug. "You could have broken your legs coming through my window, and then where would we be?"

Zachary ignored her question as he pushed her down, his cock already bulging against his trousers and desperate for release. Helene slapped his hand away. Zachary looked confused and gave her bottom a sharp spank, causing Helene to whimper.

"No, Zachary, don't you dare make love to me. We have to wait until our wedding night."

"Why?" He looked generally confused. "You're no longer a virgin. Haven't been for a while. I had the honor of taking your virginity months ago."

She rolled her eyes. "Still. I want some aspects of my wedding to remain traditional. Please. It's important to me."

He let out a groan but reluctantly agreed. Before Helene could thank him, he pushed her down on the bed. "Zachary!" He spread her legs open, her nightgown becoming tangled around her waist.

"Relax, honey. I will keep my promise, but I am already here. I might as well give you some pleasure."

Before Helene could ask what he meant by that, he pressed his face between her legs. She felt his warm breath on her privates, his facial hair rubbing the insides of her thighs.

Helene let out a small shriek when she felt his tongue part her lower lips open. The muscle felt strong and wet between her legs. This was the first time he had pleasured her with his tongue and she had no idea how pleasurable it was.

No wonder he liked seeing her on her knees often.

Zachary slapped the back of her thigh. "Relax, honey. They will hear you."

She squeaked a reply, praying she could contain herself. Her soon-to-be husband continued to pleasure her with his tongue. He licked every nook and cranny of her nether region, his tongue coating sections which made her blush.

Zachary then alternated between fucking her between her dewy lower lips and sucking on her swollen clit. Helene's entire lower body trembled with pleasure as she focused on the way he was trying to make her come. Zachary managed to squeeze two orgasms out of her before he let her rest.

Helene lay back on the bed with flushed cheeks and perspiration clinging onto her body, but with a content look on her face. The idea that her future husband always managed to make her happy in the marriage bed made her very pleased.

He kissed the tip of her nose. "Until tomorrow, my wife."

Chapter 14

"**O**h, darling, you look absolutely beautiful."

Helene didn't think she had ever seen her mother so happy. Usually, her mother seemed a little lost whenever she dealt with Helene. Corinne had always been her pride and joy and Audrina had always been meek. But Helene had always done what she wanted, even if it meant going behind her mother's back, so Mrs. Hollis had never bonded with her youngest daughter. Though Helene knew her mother loved her in her own way. Who knew, perhaps she would relax now that she was properly married.

"Do you really think so, Mother?" Helene couldn't stop staring at herself in the mirror, hardly believing the bride she saw on the other end was her.

Mrs. Hollis squeezed her arm. "You make me a proud mother, Helene. Zachary won't be able to take his eyes off you."

Helene's dress was heavily ornate and heavy, being held up with a hoop skirt and what felt like half a dozen petticoats. The shade of the dress was a luminous pearl color that Miss Belle had ordered from somewhere in Germany which made her look like a shining star. The dress had long, tight sleeves, with little flower embroidery at the cuffs while the bodice was decorated in pearls shaped like tiny flowers. Mrs. Hollis had even lent her a diamond and pearl choker that all Hollis women, with the exception of Audrina, had worn on their wedding day.

Her bright red hair was pulled up in an elegant updo with curls cascading across her ears and lightly down her back. The veil was set on top of her head, held up by a matching pearl and diamond hair comb which was dreadfully heavy.

Pink cheeks and swollen lips from the kiss Zachary stole yesterday stared back at her. Helene had never felt more beautiful. She was getting married to the man who had been her first, well, everything.

"Are you ready?" Mrs. Hollis cleared her throat, afraid that she might cry before the ceremony. "We can't keep your father and the groom waiting for too long."

Before Helene could answer, a knock was heard and the Hollis butler appeared, looking flustered.

"What is it?" Mrs. Hollis snapped.

"They've asked for you and Miss Hollis to come downstairs."

"Who asked you?"

"I'd rather not say. They said it was to be a surprise."

Mrs. Hollis let out a frustrated sigh while the butler looked like he was worried he would be fired, even though he had been working for the Hollis family for twenty-seven years.

Helene touched her mother's hand gently. "Let's just go downstairs, Mother. We're finished here and we don't want to be even more late than we already are."

"All right, darling, but if this is your father's lousy idea of a joke, then I will be cross with him."

The two women headed down the Hollises' grand staircase. When Helene found out what was waiting at the bottom of the stairs, her heart stopped inside her chest. Mother was the first to react as she let out a loud shriek.

Her sisters, along their husbands and children, were standing at the foot of the stairs. The children's nannies and their personal servants fluttered in the background with no one paying attention to them.

Mrs. Corinne Barrett was dressed in a tight red dress like she always was—even as a mother and wife, she refused to dress matronly. Her glossy dark hair cascaded down her pale shoulders, obviously not the least bit worried about what people would say. She had never liked her hair in frumpy updos. A necklace made of rubies and diamonds adorned her neck while her red lips pulled back in an all too familiar smirk.

In her arms, was a sleeping baby wrapped in a yellow and white blanket. Her husband, Nicholas, stood behind her protectively, looking as handsome as ever, which was why Corinne had fallen for him even though he was as charming as an ice sculpture. He was holding tightly to a little girl who would be almost two years old. The little girl looked exactly like Corinne, with sharp blue eyes and porcelain skin, indicating she would be a beauty like her mother. She was dressed in a tiny white dress with a huge pink sash around the waist and her tiny arms were around his neck.

Mrs. Audrina Darlington stood beside her, grinning proudly at her little sister, in a demure navy-blue dress. Her black hair was still short, never fully growing from when she'd had to cut it and it only reached the top of her shoulders, but she managed to pull it back with a pair of expensive-looking combs.

Her husband, Dominic, was holding their own newborn baby wrapped tightly in a blue blanket. He was a blond baby, like his father, and baby Darlington looked around curiously at the world around them. Dominic's own blond hair had grown longer in his time abroad and reached his back, but he kept it neat, in a braid.

Dominic was grinning at her like a proud older brother. She had spent the previous holidays with Audrina and Dominic in Boston and she had fond memories of them. She thought Dominic was a good husband for her much more reserved sister.

Mrs. Hollis let out a low cry and started kissing her older daughters on the cheek while Helene stood still, not believing the sight in front of her.

Corinne's laugh rang like bells. "Are you just going to stand there, Hel?"

Her question woke her up and Helene immediately hugged her. Her sister still smelled the same even after more than two years of marriage. They had sent letters frequently, but she hadn't realized how much she had missed her until this moment.

"You came in time for my wedding," she replied dumbly as Nicholas kissed the back of her hand.

"Of course." Corinne gave a little eye roll. "You are our baby sister and the last Hollis sister to get married. Did you really think we would miss it?"

"I thought the wedding invitations wouldn't arrive in time." Helene kissed Audrina on the cheek. "Zachary insisted on getting married so soon, I was afraid you would miss it."

"We didn't receive the invitations," Dominic replied,

hugging her. "Corinne insisted we must return to New York."

Corinne shrugged. "I had a feeling you would be wed soon. I didn't want to wait for an invitation."

Helene grinned, not sure what to say. She couldn't express the joy she was feeling. Helene would get married with her sisters and niece and nephews by her side. She clapped her hands together. "Thank you so much for coming."

Nicholas smiled as he put his daughter down on the floor, but the little girl clung to his trousers' leg, a cute pout on her adorable face. He placed a hand on Dominic's shoulder. "Let's head to the library. Our father-in-law wants to have a celebration toast."

Dominic nodded as he kissed Audrina on the forehead and then gave her the baby.

Mrs. Hollis looked at the antique clock by the staircase. "I am going to check with the driver to make sure he has everything he needs. You girls have fifteen minutes for any chattering and then we must leave." She looked at their daughters' and grandchildren's traveling outfits. "I do hope you change. You cannot come to the wedding wearing that."

Audrina rolled her eyes. "We will change, Mother. We'll meet you at the church, we'll just be a bit late."

Mrs. Hollis looked satisfied as she went to scold a poor servant or whoever stood in her way. No doubt she was the reason why her father had been hiding all morning.

Corinne and Audrina gushed over her expensive dress and veil for a few more minutes before Helene interrupted them. "Can we have some introductions?" She pointed to the children.

Corinne nodded as she patted her daughter's head; she

was hiding shyly behind her mother's skirt. "This is Clarissa. Clarissa, this is your Aunt Helene, say hello."

"Hello," the little girl said softly before hiding behind her mother's skirts again. She lifted her baby boy up higher. "And this is Neal."

The sleeping boy had Nicholas and Corinne's dark hair. He was even frowning in his sleep, no doubt the little angel had inherited both of his parents' awful tempers.

Audrina raised her blond son, who stared at her curiously with lovely green eyes. He had inherited every trait from his father. "And this is Malcolm. We call him Mal."

"They're so lovely." Helene touched Mal's cheek. He giggled. "I'm so happy I got to meet them, but you two shouldn't have forced yourselves to come. Both of you have just given birth and the journey must have been horrendous."

Audrina and Corinne exchanged looks before the middle sister shrugged. "It wasn't too bad. Our husbands weren't too happy with us, but we made it work. We wanted to be here for you."

"And I miss New York." Corinne tossed her hair over her shoulder. "The English countryside is not as exciting as Jane Austen makes it out to be. When Dominic and Audrina return to New York in March permanently, I shall miss them terribly."

"You have your husband," Audrina pointed out.

"He works too much," Corinne huffed. "Besides, if we were living in London, things might be different. I could attend musicals, shop, or go to art galleries. In the country, there is nothing but sheep and horses."

"At least you are far enough away from society that you don't get judged every time you use a handkerchief." Audrina shuddered. She was married to one of the richest men in New York and would be expected to take her rightful place as a New York queen once she and her husband returned from their year abroad. This was not something she was looking forward to, as she was naturally shy.

Corinne scowled, obviously not agreeing. "At least you'll have Helene living in the same city as you. I'll have no one."

"Perhaps you and the children can come over after our wedding trip for a nice, long visit," Helene offered generously.

Corinne brightened for a bit, but then she sighed. "Nicholas would never allow it. He'll miss us too much and I'd miss him."

Audrina looked surprised. "That's the first time I've heard you say you'll miss your husband. You two are usually fighting like a pair of cats."

"He's still my husband. Besides, we can't be mad at each other for long if he's managed to get me pregnant twice in less than three years." She smiled smugly. "Though I could do without his discipline every once in a while."

Helene looked surprised and she was tempted to ask her if she was also whipped by her husband when she broke a rule. She knew Audrina was. Though this was not the time nor the place. She would have to ask her sister later, before she departed.

"We do not have much time before Mother comes over to fuss." Audrina started rocking baby Mal who had started to whine, probably aching for her breast. "How did you and Zachary Easton meet? What kind of man is he? We'd danced a few times together before I married. He seems like a very nice man."

"He is a nice man. Funny too. He's Kathleen's older brother, so we used to play together when we were younger before he was shipped off to boarding school. We reunited after he graduated from Harvard at one of Mother's friend's ball."

For some reason Helene was feeling shy about how Zachary had become her teacher in anything sexual during these past few months. That was Zachary and Helene's own secret story and she preferred to keep it between them. It would make it all the more special. Something they would take to the grave.

"Is he nice to you?" Corinne asked.

"Yes."

"Then, that's all that matters."

It was such a strange thing for someone as spoiled and vain as Corinne to say, but perhaps motherhood had changed her.

Audrina kissed Helene's cheek. "We should probably let Hel get into the carriage before Mother throws a fit. We also need to get ready, Cor, and get the children to their nannies."

Clarissa stomped on her foot, a frown on her pretty face. "I wanna go! Mama, Mama, take me! Now!"

Helene sighed in amusement. It looked like Clarissa was going to be a headache like her mother had been.

Corinne leaned down so she was looking at her daughter straight in the eye. "Weddings are no place for children, darling. Now, stop behaving naughtily or I will tell Papa. We will buy you many pretty things tomorrow and take you to places Mama went to when she was a little girl. Don't you want that?"

Clarissa nodded as she patted her mother's cheek. "Rissa good."

Corinne smiled and kissed her cheek. "Now, say goodbye to Auntie Drina and Auntie Hel before you go to Nanny."

Audrina leaned down so that Clarissa could kiss her

aunt and her cousin while Corinne handed her son to their nanny who had come to pick up the children. Helene picked Clarissa up and spun her around even though she was in her heavy wedding dress, causing the girl to giggle.

"Helene, your hair!" Corinne scolded.

Helene ignored her as she kissed her niece on the cheek. "I promise you can help me and your Uncle Zachary open wedding presents tomorrow."

The girl brightened before she went scurrying to her mother.

"Are you sure you are mature enough to get married?" Audrina teased her as she and Corinne helped her tidy herself up.

Helene laughed. Audrina had married in her early twenties and Corinne not until she was twenty-four. She never thought she would get married at eighteen. She clutched the bouquet in her hands. "As ready as I will ever be."

Mrs. Hollis darted into the room, an impatient look on her face. "Girls! What is taking so long? Helene, your husband will think you deserted him if you keep him any longer."

Husband. Helene couldn't think of a sweeter word.

She winked at both of her sisters. "I will see you at the church."

The ride to the church was thankfully less than fifteen minutes. The carriage she rode in was being pulled by two fine-looking horses with glossy manes while the carriage itself was adorned with white silk ribbons and flowers.

Curious people peeked from their homes or from the streets, trying to get a glimpse of the bride. Helene felt like a royal princess.

Finally, they found themselves in front of a grand, stony church that Corinne and her parents married in.

The driver helped her out of the carriage while Kathleen waved her over. She had gone ahead to oversee a last-minute ordeal with the flowers.

Kathleen was to be her maid-of-honor, Helene didn't know any of the other girls as well and had opted for no other bridesmaids, a fact which had disappointed her mother. Kathleen was dressed in a simple blue dress which Helene had picked out because it was in her favorite hue.

"You look beautiful!" Kathleen pulled her into a hug, crushing her bouquet and causing her mother to snort in disapproval in the background. "Zachary will not be able to take his eyes off you."

"Oh, do you really think so?" She so wanted to please him, but to be honest, Zachary had never really cared much about clothes.

Kathleen nodded again before her mother scolded both of them and urged them to get themselves ready to enter the church,

Her father stood beside her with tears in his eyes and a rare moment of pride shining through. Mr. Hollis didn't have a very close relationship with his daughters. He loved them, of course, and doted on them by bringing them small gifts, but Helene always felt he saw them as puppies instead of his daughters. He had been more focused on his work than he had been on raising them, but then again, at least he hadn't been cruel.

She hoped Zachary would be a more doting father. He was a good older brother to Kathleen, so that was promising, though she and Zachary had promised each other that they wouldn't have children over the next few years. They wanted to enjoy each other's company for the time being.

There would be plenty of time for children later, though she did miss how Zachary would finish inside of her, causing that warm feeling in her belly.

"You look beautiful, sweetheart," Mr. Hollis said as he placed a noisy kiss on her cheek like he had done when she was a little girl.

"Thank you, Father."

The familiar organ music started to play as Helene and her father made their way inside. There must have been more than one hundred fifty people crowded into the church after Corinne's wedding of shame and Audrina's mysterious wedding. The crowd was ready to see a Hollis girl be properly married.

Her mother sat by herself in the first bench. If her sisters and their husbands managed to make the church ceremony, they would join her. If not, then Helene would at least see them at the wedding breakfast.

Zachary was waiting for her at the altar, dressed handsomely in a dark gray tailcoat with a matching vest and slacks. His brown hair was slicked back and his blue eyes were shining with excitement.

Zachary's second cousin stood beside him as his best man, since he didn't have many close friends, looking bored.

"Take care of her, young man." Mr. Hollis led her gently into his awaiting arms.

"I will, sir," he promised as he lifted her veil. He didn't say anything, but his smile said everything he wanted to say.

Unfortunately, the minister interrupted their sweet moment by breaking open his Bible. "Dearly beloved, we are gathered here today to unite—"

The ceremony went by quickly and before Helene knew it, she and Zachary had been declared husband and wife and they were led into the wedding carriage while the crowd clapped politely.

"We're finally married!" Helene squealed once the

carriage door was closed. She bounced in her seat from the excitement despite her heavy dress.

"I can finally call you Mrs. Easton." He kissed her softly, nibbling on her lower lip. "It felt like I would never have the chance."

"Zachary, you made Mother and me plan the wedding in a month. It's almost unheard of. People will surely think we have a baby on the way."

"Let them talk. Those nosy busybodies need something to occupy their time." Zachary squeezed her hand. "How do you feel? Do you need anything?"

"Nothing at all," Helene breathed out excitedly. "Everything is perfect."

Zachary and Helene would be leaving for their honeymoon in a week since Zachary had some business he needed to take care of. It was fine with her since she would be able to spend some time with her sisters.

They arrived at the Hollis residence where everyone would meet for the celebratory wedding breakfast. Mrs. Hollis was barking orders at the florist and the servants while Corinne and Audrina looked on with a mix of helplessness and amusement. Her father was nowhere to be seen. No doubt he had taken his sons-in-law to have a private drink in the library.

Kathleen was awkwardly holding a vase that her mother had probably shoved at her. She gave them a pained smile.

"There you two are!" Mrs. Hollis sent the nervous maid away before he approached them. "The guests will be here any minute. You two must be at the entryway in order to greet them. It will be impolite if you do not—"

"Mrs. Hollis, Cook wants to know where you would like us to put the wedding cake?"

Mrs. Hollis let out a frustrated sigh. "Honestly, I told Cook a hundred times where to put the wedding cake."

Once Mrs. Hollis left, Helene let out a little giggle. "Poor Mother, she just wants everything to be perfect, but I think everything is perfect already."

Zachary placed a hand on her hip. "Should we head upstairs to your room, my love? We both could do with some alone time before the guests bore us completely."

Helene's eyes widened. "But what about Mother?"

Zachary laughed. "She won't notice we are gone. I'll be quick."

"Not too quick." Helene gave a silent look to Corinne to warn her when Mother was coming. Corinne responded by giving her a slow wink. "Five minutes. Not a minute more and you need to be gentle. I do not want to look rumpled."

"As you wish, Mrs. Easton. I will treat you with silk gloves."

Both of them raced upstairs, Helene nearly tripping in her heavy dress.

Helene bit her lip. "Perhaps not that gentle."

Zachary laughed. "This is one of the reasons I married you, Mrs. Easton."

"Well, I married you because I love you, Mr. Easton."

Zachary leaned over to whisper in her ear, "Not as much as I love you."

Epilogue

"Welcome to Spain, my love."

Helene blinked as if she couldn't quite believe she was on Spanish soil. A few weeks ago, she had been a newlywed bride surrounded by her sisters, their husbands, and their children, and now she was in Spain with the love of her life.

She looked up at Zachary who was looking at her carefully, as if afraid of her reaction. Did he really think she wouldn't like Spain? What wasn't there to love?

Helene had only been on Spanish soil for less than an hour, but she was already sure it was her favorite place. The colors, the scent of the food, and of course, the amazing architecture she could see from their hotel room. It must be costing a fortune, but Zachary had told her to let his father worry about that.

Mr. Easton, Kathleen and Zachary's father and her new father-in-law, had been so happy his oldest son had gotten married—even if he had caused a bit of a scandal when he stole Carl Ashton's fiancée. As a wedding present, Zachary's father had paid for a six-month honeymoon trip around Europe. After Spain, they would be going to Italy and France before finishing off in England, where they would be staying with Corinne, Nicholas, and their babies, for a month.

Helene wished they never had to go home, but as Zachary pointed out gently, they had responsibilities now. He was going to take over his father's business fully once they returned from their honeymoon. Mr. Easton was tired. This was probably one of the last trips they would have without either of them having much responsibility, although Zachary promised to take her to Greece or Japan in a few years.

They hadn't discussed babies yet, but they were no longer as careful now that they were properly married. Helene knew her father-in-law was desperate for a grandchild, but she hoped that for the next few years at least, it would only be her and Zachary enjoying themselves.

"It's so lovely, I never want to leave," she declared. Helene could see a fancy, ornate Catholic church from their bedroom window. She would have to ask Zachary what it was called. She had tried learning a bit of Spanish from his travel books, but she and her husband had been too busy making love so that none of the studying had stuck.

Zachary thanked the young man who had brought their luggage upstairs before giving him a coin. Once they were alone, Zachary wrapped his large arms around his wife before placing a kiss on her cheek.

"You've hardly seen it, Hel. Perhaps you'll like France, Italy, or England more."

"England is too cold and rainy; Corinne complains about it all the time."

"Corinne complains about everything. I'm surprised Nicholas hasn't gone mad being with her all the time."

"Be nice. She's my sister. Besides, Nicholas must like her if he has two children with her." Helene giggled as she snuggled deeper into him. If she didn't end up pregnant on this trip, it would be a miracle. It seemed she and her husband could hardly keep their hands off each other. "And I'm sure Spain will be my favorite. It's so nice and warm."

"You won't be saying that when you're sweating through your clothes." Zachary playfully nibbled on her earlobe. Zachary liked biting her everywhere now that they were officially married—her neck, inner thighs, and earlobe were among his favorite places.

Helene often had to remind him that she got bruises and marks easily on her fair skin. The last thing she wanted was to be subjected to embarrassing questions.

"What do you want to do first, Helene?" Zachary murmured in her ear. "We could dine on an early dinner or perhaps see one of the famous churches nearby."

Mrs. Easton let out a girlish chuckle. "Mr. Easton, if you were truly interested in sightseeing, then you wouldn't be groping me, would you?"

"I will do whatever you want me to do, wife," Zachary promised, but his fingers were already pulling down the bodice of her navy-blue gown, exposing her pale breasts. "I am under your command, Mrs. Easton."

Helene giggled as she whispered in her husband's ear, "Then undress me, Mr. Easton. Give me another one of your famous lessons."

Annabelle Marin

Annabelle Marin is a twenty-something romantic who lives in sunny California. When she isn't writing she enjoys daydreaming, watching way too much TV, and cuddling with her pets.

Her books are sweet erotic romances with domestic discipline. In her books you can expect: a spoonful of sweetness, a dash of sass, a cup of naughtiness, and an abundance of romance.

You can follow Annabelle on Facebook, Instagram, Goodreads, and Bookbub for exciting updates on upcoming books!

Facebook-https://www.facebook.com/annabelle.marin.940/
Instagram-https://www.instagram.com/missannabellemarin/
Bookbub-//www.bookbub.com/profile/annabelle-marin
Goodreads-www.goodreads.com/author/show/21061973.Annabelle_Marin

Don't miss these exciting titles by Annabelle Marin and Blushing Books!

Stand Alone Titles

Endless Paradise

Between Kisses & Lies
Letters to Holly
On the Dotted Line
His Southern Belle

Earthly Mates Series
The Alien's Mate

The Benningtons Series
Holy Matrimony
Strawberry Kiss

The Hollis Sisters Series
The Affair
The Scandal
The Passion

The Stevenson Brothers Series
The Rancher Orders a Bride
The Pastor Takes a Wife
The Sheriff Finds a Fiancée

Vintage Beauties Series

Bless Her Heart
Becoming a Gibson Girl
The Modern Housewife
Vintage Beauties Collection

The Bride Series

The Unwilling Mrs.
The Unattainable Bride
The Unexpected Wife

Anthologies

12 Naughty Days of Christmas 2021

Blushing Books

Blushing Books is one of the oldest eBook publishers on the web. We've been running websites that publish spanking and BDSM related romance and erotica since 1999, and we have been selling eBooks since 2003. We hope you'll check out our hundreds of offerings at http://www.blushingbooks.com.

Blushing Books Newsletter

Please join the Blushing Books newsletter
to receive updates & special promotional offers.
You can also join by using your mobile phone:
Just text BLUSHING to 22828.